VIRAGO
MODERN CLASSICS
104

Emilie Rose Macaulay

Emilie Rose Macaulay (1881–1958) was born in Rugby, Warwickshire. She was educated at Oxford High School for Girls and Somerville College, Oxford, where she read Modern History. She wrote her first novel, *Abbots Verney* in 1906 whilst living in Great Shelford, near Cambridge. Rose became an ardent Anglo-Catholic and here her childhood friendship with Rupert Brooke matured and through him she was introduced to London literary society. She moved to London and in 1914 published her first book of poetry, *The Two Blind Countries*. In 1918 she met the novelist and former Catholic priest Gerald O'Donovan, the married man with whom she was to have an affair lasting until his death. Her last and most famous novel, *The Towers of Trebizond* (1956) was awarded a James Tait Black Memorial prize and became a bestseller in America. She was created a Dame Commander of the British Empire in the 1958 New Year's Honours, but seven months later suffered a heart attack and died at her home.

THE WORLD MY WILDERNESS

Rose Macaulay

*With an Introduction
by Penelope Fitzgerald*

A *Virago* Book

Published by Virago Press 1983

Reprinted 1992, 1993, 1997

First published in Great Britain by William Collins Ltd 1950, Virago
edition offset from this first edition

A CIP catalogue record for this book is available
from the British Library

ISBN 0 86068 340 0

Printed and bound in Great Britain by
Clays Ltd, St Ives plc

Virago
A Division of
Little, Brown and Company (UK)
Brettenham House
Lancaster Place
London WC2E 7EN

The world my wilderness, its caves my home,
Its weedy wastes the garden where I roam,
Its chasm'd cliffs my castle and my tomb. . . .

ANON

And bats with baby faces in the violet light
Whistled, and beat their wings
And crawled head downward down a blackened wall,
And upside down in air were towers
Tolling reminiscent bells that kept the hours,
And voices singing out of empty cisterns and exhausted wells.

In this decayed hole among the mountains
In the faint moonlight, the grass is singing
Over the tumbled graves, about the chapel,
There is the empty chapel, only the wind's home.
It has no windows, and the door swings . . .

THE WASTE LAND, *T. S. Eliot*

INTRODUCTION

Rose Macaulay was born in 1881, and died in 1958. As a young woman she went bathing by moonlight with Rupert Brooke, and she lived long enough to protest, as a well-known author and critic, against the invasion of Korea. *The World my Wilderness* was published in 1950, when she was thought to have given up fiction, not having written a novel for nearly ten years.

The book disturbed her readers, because it was not what they expected. The most successful of her early novels had been social satires. They were delightful to read, and still are, brilliantly clear-sighted without being malicious (or at least more malicious than necessary) but they took a detached view; humanity was so misguided that one must either laugh or cry, and Rose had felt it best to laugh. *The World my Wilderness* showed that the power of ridicule, after all, was not the most important gift she had.

Rose Macaulay herself was most characteristically English, tall, angular, and given to wearing flat tweed caps, or hats like tea cosies — English, too, in her gaiety and wit which, at heart, was melancholic. But almost any conclusion you came to about her would be wrong. From the ages of six to thirteen she had grown up with her brothers and sisters in a small fishing town on the Genoese coast, and this interlude of scrambling about the Mediterranean hills and foreshore was as important to her as all her English education. Again, Rose was often thought to be sexless, or, as Rosamond Lehmann put it, "sexless though not unfeminine". But in fact she had, at the age of thirty-six, fallen irretrievably in love with a married man, Gerald O'Donovan, and in spite of much heart-searching she never broke with her lover till the day of his death. Both these episodes have a good deal to do with the writing of *The World my Wilderness*.

The book's seventeen-year-old heroine Rose herself described as "rather lost and strayed and derelict". Barbary Deniston has grown up in wartime Occupied France, only half attended to by her worldly, sensual charmer of an English mother. This mother, Helen, has been divorced from Deniston, and her second husband, "an amiable, thriving French collaborator", is dead. Meanwhile Barbary and her stepbrother have lived in and out of the house as children of the Maquis, trained by the Resistance in sabotage and petty thieving. Like Auden's boy with a stone, Barbary has never heard of any world where promises were kept. When she is sent from her fishing village to the respectable Deniston relatives in London, she is doubly lost. Like seeking like, she escapes from pallid WC2 to join the drifters and scroungers in the bombed area round St Paul's, where "shrubs and green creeping things ran about a broken city." "Here, its cliffs and chasms seemed to say, is your home; here you belong; you cannot get away, you do not wish to get away, for this is the *maquis* that lies about the margins of the wrecked world." Ironically enough she begins house-keeping at once, tidying and cleaning the gaping ruins of a church. She is not a wanderer by nature, it is only that she needs a home that she can trust.

In Rose Macaulay's earlier novels, notably *Crewe Train* (1926) and *They Were Defeated* (1932), there are young girls of Barbary's sort, precociously adult, and yet clinging for reassurance to childhood. Many have names which could be either masculine or feminine, (Denham, Julian, Evelyn), as though rejecting all society's definitions. All of them are unwilling exiles from some lost paradise. They remember sunshine and freedom, as Rose remembered her Italy. But in this story of the nineteen forties, the world that Barbary longs for and looks back to is a black-marketing France. The paradise itself is corrupt. And the civilisation to which she is packed off is an equally shabby affair. Deniston, the honourable man, is an odd man out in post-war London. His son Richie describes himself as a "gentle, civilised, swindling crook", who by bending the law a little — as all his friends do — hopes to make himself a comfortable life. Barbary is no doubt right, on the beach at Collioure, to examine the word *civilisation* "and to reject it, as if it were mentioned too late". In any society, she will remain a barbarian. The novel's painful question is: what have we done to our children?

The war years had brought deep personal trouble to Rose. In 1939 she was responsible for a serious car crash in which her lover was injured. In 1941 her flat was bombed and she lost nearly everything she possessed. In 1942 Gerald O'Donovan died, and Rose entered her own waste land of remorse. How much could be forgotten, and how much could she forgive herself? In spite of this, or more probably because of it, she is more compassionate in this novel than in any other. To be self-satisfied, to be stupid, to be cruel (Rose had always said) is undesirable, if we are to consider ourselves civilised, but at the same time she was not at all easily shocked. Asked on one occasion by a question-master whether she would prefer death or dishonour she replied: "Dishonour, every time." And *The World my Wilderness* is remarkable for the pleas in mitigation she makes for all her characters. Helen has no conscience, it seems to have been left out of her, but she creates pleasure for others. Deniston is stiff, bland and resentful, but his integrity must count for something. Richie is a young aesthete who prefers to withdraw rather than to be too much involved, but then he has been fighting through three years of "messy, noisy and barbaric war". Mrs Cox, the housekeeper, can't distinguish — which of us can? — between interference and what, to her, are good intentions. Even Pamela, Deniston's second wife, wholesome tweedy Pamela ("all Pamela's clothes were good, of the kind known as cheaper in the end") — Pamela the young committeewoman, not at all Rose's favourite kind of person, redeems herself by suffering with dignity. If there is a responsibility to judge these people the author is asking us to share it.

In the same way, every turn of the story brings a different confrontation, genial against sceptical, honourable against amoral, will against emotion, rough against smooth, wild against tamed. And these encounters, too, are left unresolved. In the closing chapters, for instance, Helen comes back to London. At the Denistons' house she takes command, a supremely inconvenient guest. Her motives, as we have to admit, are generous. But poor Pamela has to hold her own against the sumptuous intruder. The contest of possessiveness, jealousy, and genuine love is so finely balanced that most readers would be hard put to it to say exactly where their sympathies lie. Rose has written the novel in terms of comedy, but all the satirist's air of knowing what's best for everybody has gone. Indeed there is, perhaps, no "best" for any of them.

Rose Macaulay liked to insist that ideas for novels came to her as places — "backgrounds" would hardly be a strong enough word for them. In *The World my Wilderness* (if we take the "respectable, smoke-dark houses" of London as a kind of negation of place) we have three of them — Collioure in the South of France, Arshaig in the Western Highlands, and the wilderness itself. Each corresponds to its own moral climate. Collioure is described in the most seductive terms. "The cool evening wind rustled in the cork forest, crept about the thymey *maquis*; the sea, drained of light, was a wash of blue shadow, sparked by the lights of fishing boats putting out for the night's catch." By day, the Villa Fraises offers serene warmth and relaxation for all comers, but always with a hint of excess. The garden is "crowded", Helen "lounged her days away", the most striking of her pictures is "a large nude who was a French mayor, reclining on a green sofa with a blue plate of strawberries in his hand; the flesh tones were superb". Arshaig is equally beautiful, but austere, with misty dawns and steel-pale water, and at the shooting lodge are a whole family of Barbary's relations, "formidably efficient at catching and killing Highland animals". But in saying this Rose reminds us that there has also been killing and hunting — of men as well as animals — in the forests of Collioure, "savageries without number", from the days of the Saracens to the Gestapo and the Resistance. And on the beach there Barbary and Raoul had stood watching the fish in the nets as they struggled, leaped and died.

Barbary herself becomes a creature of the wilderness, the ruins of the city of London. In 1950 the rubble was still lying where it had fallen, carpeted with weeds and inhabited by rats and nesting birds. The whole area fascinated Rose — how much, can be felt in the lyrical opening to Chapter Eighteen. To her they were the new catacombs. "I spent much of today in the ruins round St Paul's, which I like . . . part of my new novel is laid in this wrecked scene" she wrote to Gilbert Murray.* Many people must still remember, as I do, the alarming experience of scrambling after her that summer (she made no distinction of age on her expeditions) and keeping her spare form just in view as she shinned undaunted down a crater, or leaned, waving, through the smashed glass of some perilous window. Foxgloves, golden charlock and loosestrife were flourishing everywhere they could take root in the stones, but Rose did not sentimentalise over the wild flowers. It was not man's business, in her view, to abandon what he has won from nature. She was studying obliteration.

Descended from historians, trained as a historian herself, she makes the ruins into something more than a metaphor

* quoted in Constance Babington Smith, *Rose Macaulay* (1972)

for Barbary's desolate state; they give the novel a dimension in time. They are still alive with the indignation of all the generations who have lived and done business in the city, or worshipped in its fallen churches. "The ghosts of churches burnt in an earlier fire, St Olave's and St John Zachary's, the ghosts of taverns where merchants and clerks had drunk" all haunt their old precincts, even under the midday sun, so do the long-dead clerics and shopkeepers themselves. When Barbary is on the run, the phantoms of five centuries of London crowd together to watch, from their vanished buildings, the pitiful end of the chase. They are not sympathetic, they want her caught. History, as might be expected, is on the side of authority.

At the end of the book Richie is seen alone on the brink of the "wrecked scene", and the squalor in front of him makes him feel sick. He reflects that "we are in rat's alley, where the dead men lost their bones", quoting *The Waste Land*, from which Rose took one of the novel's epigraphs (she wrote the first one herself). But *The Waste Land* is also a fitful quest for spiritual healing, and Richie, in the end, takes the track from Moorgate Station "across the wilderness towards St Paul's". This is one of several hints in the book of a religious solution, or, at least, of curiosity about one, even though Barbary and Raoul perceive that "if there is anything, there must be hell. But one supposes there is nothing."

The World my Wilderness is, in fact, not a pessimist's book — heartfelt, yes, but pessimistic, no. However faulty the main characters may be, there is one striking fact about them; their mistakes are not the result of caring nothing about each other, but of caring too much. It is because he still loves Helen that Deniston fails to forgive her, and Helen herself learns in the end not only how much she loves her daughter, but a way to help her. "She must have sunshine, geniality, laughter, love; and if she goes to the devil she shall at least go happily, my little savage." This is probably the best that Helen can do. And if the inhabitants of this earth, in spite of the mess, the slaughter and the desolation they cause, can give up so much for each other, they must be redeemable. In the last resort, Rose Macaulay thought so. And she was, as her novel shows, too much interested in human beings to lose faith in them.

Penelope Fitzgerald, London, 1982

* 1 *

THE villa, facing south, stood above the little town and
port, on the slope between the sea and the Forêt de
Sorède. It was strawberry pink, with green shutters shaped
like leaves, and some green bogus windows and shutters,
with painted ladies looking out of them, but most of the
windows were real, and had balconies full of shrubs and
blue pots and drying bathing suits and golden cucumbers
in piles. There was a flat terraced roof with vine trellises
on it, and outside the villa stone steps climbed up to the
roof. The garden was crowded with shrubs and flowers
and orange and lemon trees, and pomegranates and
magnolias and bougainvilleas and vines. A veranda ran
across the south front of the house; behind it were the
long, cool, shady rooms, with whitewashed walls and floors
of small glossy dark-red tiles, spread with bright striped
mats. The walls of the largest room were painted with a
dado of sea and creatures of the deep, such as dolphins,
tritons, mermaids eating honey-comb, sea horses and gaily
striped fish. There were a few modern paintings; the
most imposing was a large nude who was a French mayor,
reclining on a green sofa with a blue plate of strawberries
in his hand; his flesh tones were superb. This nude, whose

7

name was Charles Michel, had been the builder and first owner of the Villa Fraises, but was now dead. So was his son Maurice, the second owner, who had collaborated mildly but prosperously from 1940 to 1945, and had thereafter been found drowned in the bay, leaving the Villa Fraises in the possession of his English wife, an artist who had painted the pictures in the room, and had lived with him in it since the fall of France had left her stranded with her ten years old daughter at Collioure.

Owing to having collaborated, however mildly, the Michels had lived quite well, and had been able to ameliorate also the lives of many of their neighbours, including some of the local maquis, but the maquis, a thankless tribe, had held this against them when the hour struck and the liberating troops swept into Provence. The Villa Fraises was under a cloud; after its owner's death, his widow had been spared retribution owing to her having more than once sheltered escaped allied prisoners waiting to cross the Pyrenees, and to the well-meant, if somewhat jejune, activities of her daughter and stepson in the juvenile fringes of the maquis. Still, as relict of the collaborating M. Michel, who was suspected (unjustly) of having betrayed fugitives and resistance members to the Vichy police in Perpignan in return for petrol and other conveniences, Madame Michel had found herself in an embarrassing position. Fortunately she was not easily embarrassed.

A large, handsome, dissipated, detached and idle woman, more interested in classical literature and the pleasures of the gaming table than in painting, which, she found, demanded more application than she was prepared, in these days, to

8

exert, she was inclined to lounge her days away, playing any game for any stakes with any one at hand, idly translating Greek comedies into French, playing with her infant son, or merely reading for pleasure. On this mid-April afternoon she lay in a hammock in the garden, among oleanders and statues, while the mother of Maurice Michel, who was paying a visit to the Fraises, sat erect and black-weeded on the veranda, netting. Madame Michel was thin and patriotic; she had curled white hair and a tight mouth; the generous, ample curves, the lounging ease, the brightly-coloured clothes, the absorption in literature and in games of chance, of the bereaved mistress of her son, she found exasperating. (As his mistress she still regarded her daughter-in-law, since she had a husband still alive in London.) And more than exasperating that Maurice had left her the Fraises. Madame Michel, a good anglophobe, disliked the British, who lacked literature, culture, language and manners, had run away from the boches in 1940 and left France to face them, and now gave themselves the airs of liberators, when any liberating that had not been done by the French themselves had been the work of the Americans. Nor did Madame Michel care for Helen's pictures; she particularly disliked the nude mayor, her late husband, a fancy portrait which had, with the aid of a photograph and of Maurice's descriptions, achieved a startling likeness. It was characteristic of Maurice to have permitted and enjoyed this portrait; it had been to him, his mother felt, the reaffirmation of the alliance he had always had with his jolly, ribald father against her, for whom he had never much cared. For Maurice had all his life liked jolly, ribald people. He had not much liked his first wife, a girl from a convent school with whom he had made a marriage of convenience at the age of thirty, and whose brief life he had never permitted unduly to hamper his own. He had seen her features and expression repeated in their son Raoul, who had always, therefore, a little irritated him. His own, on the other hand, were evident in the infant Roland. It was to arrange for Raoul's future that his grandmother was, and how reluctantly, visiting the Villa Fraises.

" And where," inquired Madame Michel, her sharp voice, speaking the French of Bordeaux, sawing the slumbrous, syringa-sweet garden air like the zirring of crickets, " is Raoul all this afternoon ? "

" I don't precisely know." The voice from the hammock was deep, slow, lazy, and spoke the French of the ateliers of the rive gauche, where its owner had picked it up as a girl. " He and Barbary—they are out together with their friends from morning till night, and often from night till morning. They are probably out with the fishing boats."

" You permit it to your daughter, Madame ? " Her son's mistress had not, in six years, advanced into a closer intimacy than this; she remained madame, and *vous*.

" I ? " The languid voice sounded faintly surprised. " I don't interfere with Barbary. She is seventeen, you know."

Madame, pursing her lips, uttered a sound like " psst." It was apparent that she did not regard seventeen as an age when a daughter should not be interfered with.

" It is just as well, Madame, that you are sending that young girl to England."

" I supposed that her father might like to have her with him for a time."

" It is only natural. And you? You will not take her to England yourself? "

" No. Her brother is coming out to see me, and they will return together."

" Ah." Madame Michel, clicking her needles rapidly, absorbed the situation. This woman would stay on at the Fraises. She had no intention of visiting her native land; she was divorced, disgraced, her husband in London (a well-known lawyer, Madame Michel had heard), had re-married. There seemed, really, no reason why she should ever leave the Fraises. Madame Michel herself preferred to live at Bordeaux, where she had her house and her position as widow of a respected mayor; but she could have let the Fraises to good advantage. Her voice took a sharper edge of acerbity.

" And Raoul? "

" Ah, Raoul." His stepmother's voice was detached, expressionless, perhaps a little bored. " We must make a plan for Raoul, to be sure. It is for you to say, Madame, what Raoul is to do. If you think it well that he should stay on here, and continue his schooling at the Lycée. . . ."

" It would not be well at all."

" No? I am inclined to agree with you. During the last years, Raoul has rather occupied himself with *les enfants du maquis* than with the Lycée. He still does so, and so does Barbary. The young people regard it as a kind of club, and now that the war is over, it still absorbs them."

"What is it that they do together now, the young people?"

"Annoy the gendarmerie and the local authorities. Steal when they can; trespass on private property; sabotage motor cars; molest their fellow citizens. The same activities, in fact, that they pursued from patriotism during the war, they still pursue now from inclination and force of habit."

"But it is shocking, all that." Madame Michel was startled, all her bourgeois instincts and principles of propriety outraged.

"Maurice," she added, indignant, half-incredulous, "permitted it?"

"Maurice. . . ." Maurice's wife lay motionless, her hands locked behind her head; her voice trailed away. Had Maurice permitted it? Had Maurice known how closely the two children were involved? How they would every afternoon, every evening after leaving the Lycée, every Sunday and holiday, go up into the hills or down to the shore, meeting their companions, playing their secret games, hanging round the fringes of the real grown-up maquis, who went about their secret, dangerous business in the foothills of the Pyrenees?

"Maurice supposed they were out playing. Boy Scouts, Girl Guides," she added in English. "Red Indians."

Madame Michel did not admit any of these uncouth savages into her world, the world of what it was correct for *les jeunes gens* to do.

"They must surely," she suggested, "have been sometimes in trouble with the police."

" Often, naturally."

It was apparent that the young people had disgraced themselves and their respective parents, which was what one would have expected. Certainly the sooner they left the neighbourhood the better. Madame Michel had already made her plan for Raoul, who would be too troublesome for the Bordeaux ménage.

" My son and his wife in London are willing to have Raoul for the present. He has a business in the city. Raoul can live there, and go to school. It will be better that he should be out of France, where there is so much misfortune and so little to eat. We want him to learn English business, where there may later be an opening for him, if his uncle thinks him suitable. We understand that in England, since it was almost untouched by the war, there is much prosperity."

England, she thought, always came well out of every war, losing neither lives nor money, while France was bled white.

" My son," she went on, " can arrange for his *permit de séjour*. If he could travel to England with your son and daughter, it would perhaps be convenient."

" By all means. My son will be here in a fortnight, and will return to England with his sister a few days after that. Barbary will like to have Raoul with her."

" You will miss your daughter, Madame ? "

Madame Michel was coldly polite to this objectionable, unrespectable Englishwoman, who seemed to consider the question before replying.

" No, not really. No."

Not even fond of her child. Madame Michel had guessed as much, after seeing the two together the evening before.

But now the child arrived, coming up the garden from the path that led down to the shore, Raoul at her heels. She looked childish for her age, small, with bare brown legs, a short pink print frock, draggled and wet, a prawning net trailing from her hand, a colourless, irregular, olive face, full, rather sulky mouth, fine broad forehead, flaggy dark hair, unwaved, perhaps unkempt, flapping about her neck, slanting, secret grey eyes that looked aside, looked often on the ground under a dark, frowning line of brow; something defensive, puzzled, wary about her, like a watchful little animal or savage. The boy, two years younger, had a touch of the same expression; but he looked French, and quick, perhaps clever, nearer to civilisation, as if it might one day catch hold of him and keep him, whereas the girl would surely be out of the trap and away, running uncatchable for the dark forest. Raoul too was slight and small, olive and pale; his eyes were large, a clear brown; his features were neater and prettier than Barbary's; as has been mentioned, he looked like his girl mother, who had bored her husband, and her husband's parents, a good deal. His grandmother supposed that the untidy little *gamine* Barbe led him into much mischief. He too was wet, and smelt of fish.

" Good evening, my child." Madame Michel put down her netting and surveyed him sharply over her glasses. " We have not seen you all day, I think, have we ? "

" No, grand'mère." He assented civilly, without interest, as to a self-evident proposition.

"Well, we must make up for it to-morrow, must we not? I have a great deal to say to you, my child. To-morrow you and I will have a long talk."

"Yes, grand'mère." The clear brown eyes flickered and blinked; he looked at once apprehensive and shifty. His grandmother reflected that he knew nothing yet of what his future was to be; he was in her hands, and for a moment she felt the gratification of the power she had never had over the silent, convent-bred girl, her son's wife.

"But now," she added, with some sharpness, "you must go and get dry and tidy. It appears to me that you should ask the pardon of madame for going into her house in that state."

Her eyes glanced in passing at the bedraggled girl at her grandson's side, at the wet prawning net silver with fish, at the bare sandy legs. Her gaze travelled over the unkempt figure to the large woman in the hammock, lounging with her book in one hand, her cigarette smouldering in its long amber holder in the other. She caught the thoughtful, withdrawn, disengaged look that rested on the girl and boy; and, glancing back at the girl, saw an expression in the sullen grey eyes that perplexed her.

Helen lazily waved aside the question of asking pardon.

"The house is used to it, dear madame. We all enter it wet all day."

"We've got some fish, mother." Barbary spoke in English, husky and shy, showing her net. Helen answered in French.

"So I see, Barbary. You had better give them to Marthe, if you want them for supper."

15

"Oui, ma mère." The net was withdrawn, with the family intimacy of the English language.

"If Marthe is still upstairs with Roland, don't interrupt her," Helen added. "I don't want him excited before he sleeps."

"Bien, ma mère."

The girl and boy went in through the open French windows, padding wetly over the rugs and red tiles.

She does not love the young girl, Madame Michel reflected, without surprise. She only loves the little one, who so much resembles Maurice. The thought gave her a pang of jealousy; she felt excluded by one generation after another from the circle of jolly companionship. The child Roland, looking slyly up at her with his father's merry little eyes, his grandfather's fat chuckle, snuggling his bullet head against his mother's knee, carried on the Michel male tradition of who knew what of libertinage and coarse, licentious mirth; a tradition in which his mother too stood. His grandmother, inimically outside it, regarded it with frosty discontent.

"You don't care, Madame, that Roland should run about with the other two?" she probed. "You think they would take him into mischief."

"It seems not impossible," Helen agreed, with her *dégagé* negligence. "In any case, he is too little. He would get tired. They and their friends live at a great pace, running about the hills and shore. Roland plays by the sea with me or with Marthe. I am teaching him to swim."

"Already? He is young for that."

"Even babies should know how to swim."

Maurice, his mother remembered, had not swum much ; he had been a shore bather.

Helen got up from the hammock. It could be seen that she was a large woman, long-legged, with the low, full breasts, the firm, robust waist and dignified hips of the Milo Venus, the neck a strong, rounded column, supporting a fine massive dark head and classical features, full-chinned, straight nosed, with wide, sensual mouth and quizzical eyes. In a Greek-Iberian head-dress with great studded ear-wheels, she would have been, almost, the Lady of Elche; but had a trifle more of amusement, a good deal less of mysticism, in her narrower-lidded tawny eyes and large curled mouth. She had beauty, Madame Michel grudgingly admitted; the kind of firm handsomeness that, in the forties, persists, unfaded, unwrinkled, unfallen, and still with its magnolia bloom. Neither her daughter, an irregular-featured elf, nor her son, a dumpling charmer, would have this handsomeness. Madame Michel wondered if the elder son, who was coming out in a fortnight, had it; she believed not, from a snapshot group she had seen in a writing-case, in which he, a schoolboy of seven or eight years ago, appeared, a slight, flannelled figure with raised, quizzical eyebrows and oval face, standing by his sharp-featured, distinguished-looking father, while the nine-year-old imp Barbary, in jersey and shorts, her hair tumbling into her eyes, leaned against her mother, holding tightly on to the large hand that lay on her shoulder, looking up with a confident grin. It was curious, thought Madame Michel, that Barbary in that group had the air of being her mother's darling. Ah well, between nine and seventeen there occurs adolescence,

17

that tiresome and awkward age, in which the young girl still floundered, angular, leggy and shy like a colt; a colt somehow lost and strayed; the adjective *égaré* crossed Madame Michel's unsympathetic but shrewd mind. She was not fond of *jeunes filles*; they had to occur, but the sooner they burgeoned into the married state for which the good God had created them, the better. Since, obviously, no sensible man would be likely to entertain the project of marrying Barbary, a *jeune fille* she would no doubt remain, until such time as she would wither into a *vieille fille*, of, Madame Michel anticipated, most dubious morals; she would in all probability be more disreputable than her mother, who had, at least, been twice a wife.

These speculations about Helen and her family streaked rapidly through the hard and acute mind of Madame Michel during the moment in which her daughter-in-law lounged, lithe and massive like a stretching animal, from the garden to the veranda.

"I am going up to see Roland," she said, and went into the cool house.

The abode of Roland was a pleasant room, its white walls decorated by his mother with a series of painted animals; if Roland should weary of any of these they would be washed out and replaced by others. Roland's cot was low and white, with pink blankets, and in it lay Roland asleep, his toy dog and horse beside him, his globular cheek a pink balloon against the pillow, for his mother was not of those who force infants to lie pillowless and flat. The room was dim; in the first moment she did not see Barbary crouched by the cot, still in her wet frock, her draggled hair drooping

18

like dank seaweed round her face. She got up, startled, defensive, pushing her hair from her eyes.

" I didn't disturb him," she whispered. " I only wanted to look at him. . . ."

Helen gave her across the sleeping child her withdrawn, enigmatic glance, the glance that had puzzled Madame Michel.

" You had better change into something drier," she murmured, and added, " I should think," as if it were actually no concern of hers if Barbary were wet or dry.

For a moment Barbary paused, a hesitant shadow in the shadowed room. Her lips moved, forming a word—mother, mummy, it might have been; but now Helen's glance had left her, she was leaning over Roland picking him up to set him on his pot. Replacing him, she straightened the blanket, arranged the toys, touched his cheek with her finger to feel if he was too hot, made the little adjustments that one makes in the night lives of infants lest some ill befall them before morning, such as hanging upside down, or rolling from their couches, or tossing off their bed-clothes, or smothering themselves beneath them, or lying on a toy. Roland was a placid and cheerful sleeper; not like Barbary had been at his age, all nerves, waking in terror, screaming at shadows, then, when her mother arrived, hiding her face in her breast, and clutching her with both arms. Barbary had been a wild baby, a nervy, excited child, her mother her tower of refuge. Roland needed no refuge; he was the jolly, buccaneering captain of his own soul. He distributed his favours like a cheerful courtesan. He loved his mother dearly, Marthe quite

19

sufficiently, Barbary very much, Raoul more or less, his grandmother not at all; and slept peacefully through the night till he woke with the morning light and shouted for someone to play with him. It was always Barbary who came.

Barbary slipped from the room, as quiet as a despondent breath. She and Raoul had acquired movements almost noiseless, the slinking step, the affected, furtive glide, the quick, wary glancing right and left, of jungle creatures.

Helen, having arranged her little son, braced herself for the evening with her mother-in-law, her daughter, and her stepson. How upright Madame Michel would sit, making no concessions to the ease of the Fraises chairs and couches. As to the two children, after supper they would silently steal away, to get wet and dirty all over again. During the meal, they would scarcely speak. Their manners, as Madame Michel could be seen to reflect, were *farouche* beyond reason. Fortunately to-night was her last evening at the Fraises.

* 2 *

RICHMOND DENISTON arrived from the station in a fiacre, sitting placidly like an idol under the shade of a canopy, driving through the blue and golden April morning, as trim and neat after the night journey from Paris as if he had travelled in a band-box packed round with tissue paper. He was slim, elegant and twenty-three, now in his first year at Cambridge after three years of messy, noisy and barbaric war, imprisonment, escape, adventure and victory. He was one of those returned warriors whose hang-over was not toughness, but an ardent and delighted reaction towards the exquisite niceties of civilisation. He liked luxury, the amenities of wealth and comfort, mulled claret drunk in decorative rooms lit by tall candles, the sparkle and glitter of good talk and good glass, the savour of delicate food. "The century of the common man:" ominous phrase, that he and his friends liked to turn on their tongues with relishing distaste; lacking this bogy, this sense of there being massed against them a philistine, vocal army terrible with slogans, illiterate cries, and destructive levelling aims, the young gentlemen would have been less happy, less themselves.

In appearance, Richmond Deniston was pale and fair, a

little like his father the K.C.; but gentler, milder, blander; the irony of his high-raised brows (over one of them ran a puckered scar) and sensitive mouth was more amused and tolerant, less cynical. People called him a charming boy; his father a brilliant but intimidating man. He liked both his parents very much, and wished that they had not permitted a temporary irritation and coldness, followed by what might have been merely a temporary continental escapade, to drift to a permanent breach, a breach now made irrevocable by divorce and the re-marriage of his father to a vigorous young woman named Pamela.

Helen saw him coming through the pink gate-pillars (which were crowned by stones shaped like strawberries), walking up through the sweet-smelling tangle of the garden to the veranda. She rose from the hammock to meet him. She had last seen him a year ago, when, having helped to liberate France, he had come down to Provence on a short leave. Maurice had been alive then; but what Richie, behind his pleasant manners, had thought of Maurice, she never inquired and was never told; she was not an inquisitive woman, and did not believe that such things mattered much.

They embraced with pleasure and affection. Richie, who in 1943, escaping from a German prison camp and being passed by the Resistance across France to the Spanish frontier, had visited his mother and found her the mistress of a thriving and amiable French collaborator, had in 1945 found her the collaborator's wife, and now his widow. He reflected, as she sat down again in the hammock, the table by her side littered with a miscellany of assorted

22

amusements—Greek plays, French novels, playing cards, a
chess-board, bottles and glasses—how little of a French
widow she with her deep-yellow linen dress and lounging
air appeared. She gave him a Pernod and took one herself.

"Coffee, dear child? I suppose you've had some,
though."

"Yes, at Perpignan. Well, dear mamma, how are you?"

He looked at her with his kind solicitude, his brows
lifted high in sympathy. The drowning of Maurice had
occurred last October; her letter informing him of it had
been brief and dry; he had not known, and did not expect
to know, if she greatly grieved or not.

"Very well, Richie." And so, with her serene brow and
sun-deep magnolia bloom, she appeared to be. Richie, a
young man of perceptive sensibility, knew that she had loved
Maurice. Still, he reflected, glancing at the miscellaneous
litter on the table, she had resources, she was not one of
those women who are caught by fate defenceless. Nor had
his father been caught defenceless; he had his briefs, his
cases, his legal dinners, and, before long, Pamela.

"How," Helen asked, pouring out another Pernod, "is
your father?"

"Oh, he's well. Very busy, very distinguished, very
much sought and admired. I find him, you know, more
and more delightful company. I suppose one had forgotten
how well he talked. And I suppose one appreciates it more
—not only from being grown up, but after those years in
the hangars of the Philistines. Oh, I do like being a civilian,
and at Cambridge, and with leisure to enjoy things. You
know, I don't work very much."

23

" No, I expect not. You had better work enough to get a first, hadn't you ? "

She had first instructed him in the classical tongues; at his schools, private and public, he had done well. But war, breaking in like a herd of wild beasts, tramples scholarship and the humanities underfoot; perhaps Richie had forgotten his Latin and his Greek, and had lost the aptitude to learn. Perhaps at Cambridge he led merely the dissipated life; or, vying happiness, like John Evelyn in his garden, in a thousand easy and sweet diversions, he had fallen into that condition reprehended by Richard Steele as a peril of university life, " where the youth are too apt to be lulled into a state of such tranquillity as prejudices 'em against the bustle of that worldly business for which this part of their education should prepare 'em," and " irrecoverably sunk and immers'd in the luxury of an easy-chair." This was, indeed, more or less what had occurred to Helen herself at Cambridge, and she had never quite got over it, even when labouring as an art student among the ardours of Paris.

" I suppose so," Richie answered. " If I want the F.O. It's a nuisance, rather. But I think I do want the F.O. And, anyhow, a bad degree is like a dunce's cap, whatever job you try for; people keep asking about it, and if you tell them wrong they look it up. But we returned warriors have to compete with callow young men fresh from their mother's milk and the sixth form; they know more Greek than we have ever forgotten. I don't object to them, though, if they do know some Greek; the curse of Cambridge are the ones who don't. Science or economics

24

scholars from the grammar schools. "Learning will be
cast into the mire and trodden down under the hoofs of a
swinish multitude." Burke. Such dreary accents, too. I
now go in for snobbism in a big way, mamma; I like it.
I'm a Tory, you know."

"Yes, dear, I'm sure you are. Barbary, on the other
hand, is an anarchist, like Raoul and all their maquis
friends."

"An *anarchist*? "

"Well, they don't call it that; they may think they're
communist, or anything else. Not that Barbary knows one
party from another; the child's so ignorant, she can barely
read. But, actually, they seem anarchists; they are against
all authority, and used to hiding bombs about the place
and derailing trains. It seems to have become an instinct.
Really she must drop all that nonsense in London. Her
father wouldn't like it at all."

Richie giggled. "No more he would. Nor should I.
And as to Pamela . . ."

"Oh, yes; tell me about Pamela. I remember her such
a handsome golfing girl. How is she shaping? "

"The same shape still, I think. She flourishes and
prospers and manages the house very well, and has produced
a fine son. She is very hearty and wholesome and busy
and neat, and, besides playing golf, belongs to committees
and things."

"Ah. I never did that," Helen murmured. "It leaves
one no time. Who does your stepbrother look like? "

"Pamela, I think. He looks sensible and handsome. His
name is David."

25

"Your other stepbrother looks witty and gay and rather immoral, and is getting as plump as a young tunny."

Both wondered if these two little boys would ever meet.

"Barbary," Helen went on, "dotes on Roly. Perhaps she'll dote on David. But perhaps not. She may feel jealous of him for Roly's sake, and of Pamela for mine and her own. You mustn't let them bicker."

"I don't think Pam does bicker, exactly."

"No?" An inexact word also, Helen was possibly thinking, for the way in which Barbary might behave if roused to hostility. A word too immoderate for one young woman seemed too mild for the other.

"I might," Helen said, "write to your father about Barbary."

She knew that she would not; she seldom wrote letters, never troublesome letters, and no letters at all to Sir Gulliver Deniston.

"Or perhaps not," she amended. "He might not care to hear from me. You must explain Barbary to him as best you can. She's led such a peculiar life since she was ten; really, *most* peculiar. . . . By the way, I told Raoul's grand-'mère that you would take him with you to England; he is to live with an uncle in London. She wants to get him away from the companions he goes about with here, but she doesn't want him with her at Bordeaux. His uncle or aunt will meet him at Waterloo and take him off your hands. He and Barbary, though they bicker and sulk with each other often, are inseparable here; but they'd better not meet much in London, they'd lead each other into mischief."

" You want Barbary to learn to be a young lady ? " He cocked his head sideways at her, inquisitive.

" Oh, dear no; quite impossible."

" A cricket-playing English schoolgirl, perhaps ? "

" She won't turn into that, if she goes to the Slade. She's quite clever at drawing, and daubs on her paint rather amusingly. Or rather, she did; she's dropped it lately, She'd better take to it again. She'll never learn anything else, she hasn't that kind of brain. I could never put any Latin into her, and I doubt if she absorbs much information at that Lycée. Her French, of course, is Midi, but she talks it almost as easily as English. . . . Will she get on with your father's wife ? I don't see how they could, actually."

" Well . . . get on . . ." Richie weighed the phrase, considering it. " No, I don't see them quite doing anything so actively matey as that. But they can live side by side, no doubt, without fighting. Pam's quite good humoured."

" Oh. Barbary isn't. She's such a ragamuffin, too; she'll shock everyone. Her father too."

" Father will try to civilise her. He is such a very civilised man."

" Very civilised indeed. Well, they must all manage somehow as best they can." She seemed to wash her hands of them. " It's time," she added, " that Barbary got away from here."

Richie wondered if his mother was happy among her neighbours; if they felt ill will towards her; that formidable French ill will that was still avenging itself on collaborators and suspects all over the country. He knew that, though

the Michels had more than once sheltered escaped allied
prisoners, Maurice had made money out of the Nazis, and
had accommodated himself with ease to Vichy, saying that,
since France had come to terms with Germany, it was not
for French citizens to wage a private war of their own, one
must bow to the *force majeure* and make the best of it. That
was the way Maurice had talked to Richie in '43, when
Richie and a friend had spent three days concealed at the
Villa Fraises, waiting for the maquis to guide them over
the mountains into Spain. Maurice had been kind and
genial, and had not betrayed them; he would not have
done that even if it had not been for Helen; but he had
done business with Germans, had them to his house,
rendered them services, accepted their presence with a
cheerful, contemptuous shrug. They had won, France had
lost; it was the fortune of war; what would you have?
One must behave like a civilised being, even to victorious
invaders, not lurk round them like savages in a jungle,
plotting and executing futile vengeances. The Abbé
Dinant, Maurice's friend and neighbour, had recommended
to his flock this pacific and Christian attitude; so did his
bishop; both had rebuked the Collioure curé for taking a
different line. After all, as the bishop and the abbé and
Maurice and many of his business friends agreed, though
these Nazis were barbarians and interlopers and the enemies
of France, they were at least fighting the worst enemies of
religion, civilisation and the true France, those impossible
Bolsheviks.

But Maurice was gone; and his widow seemed to be
regarded with tolerant indifference. No one could well

have cared less how she was regarded than she. All she seemed to demand of life was that she should be let alone, a comfortable, ironic hedonist, her amusements reading, painting a little (but less and less; she grew lazier, tended to go to pieces), gaming, playing chess and cards with a few friends, bathing, eating and drinking, playing with her little son, and lounging about her garden and house alone. Not the kind of life she had been able to lead in London as Lady Deniston, the wife of a busy and distinguished K.C. Quite apart from Maurice, that life had had to fall to pieces in the end.

"It's a pity," said Helen, "that I wasn't expecting you till to-morrow. The abbé is coming in after supper to play chess. But he won't, I hope, stay long."

"I don't mind. I rather like abbés. I might become a Roman Catholic one day."

"Dear child, why? What an odd notion. Are you religious?"

"Not yet. But I might go Catholic, all the same. I like their traditionalism; their high Toryism; the stand they put up against the tide. All tides, I mean. Their services are enchanting, too. What services ought to be, if they are to be at all."

"Your father always preferred King's College chapel and the Temple church. He called himself an anglo-agnostic. To me, none of them mean anything. But could you ever accept those . . . simplicities? Pilgrimages, healings, miracles, all the rest?"

"My popish friends say you don't have to ; they're not *de fide*."

" But that extraordinary creed. Yes, I know it's nearly the same as the Anglican, but one wouldn't take on the Anglican church either; one's baptized into it too young to say no. Could you really, darling? "

" I don't know. Plenty of extremely intelligent people do. But I probably shan't. I'm not religious, I'm worldly."

" Religion seems more in Barbary's line, only I think she's anti-clerical at present. I can't think, if people want gods, why not the Greek ones; they were so useful in emergencies, and such enterprising and entertaining companions. Capricious, of course, but helpful, unless one offended them. I don't know why paganism has so quite gone out in England; I suppose we're not naturally a god-fearing people. The Provençals are more; I expect it's their Italian blood. The abbé says they leave fish on stone altars in the hills; he calls it apostacy, and the heresy of the Collyridians. But he's a rather fanciful man; I expect the fish is really only the leavings of people's lunch. Now what do you want to do? Change, I suppose, first."

Richie agreed that he did, and followed his mother into the house. Helen told him he would do better to bathe in the bathroom than in the sea, which no one entered until May, or even June, it being cold in the spring. Richie said he would bathe in it all the same, and made his way down along the track that led from the garden gate to a small sandy cove beyond the port.

In the bay a boat was being rowed in to shore, trailing behind it a net. A girl and boy sat in the bows, sprawling over the sides, staring down into the green sea for fish.

Richie, swimming out into the chill waters, hailed them. The girl looked round at him, shaking her lanky hair back from her face.

"Hallo. I didn't know you were coming to-day."

The boat nosed through creaming ripples, grounding on sand. The fisherman, helped by the girl and boy, dragged in the net, with its leaping crowd of blanquettes. Richie swam in to shore ; he was cold and blue, and shivered in the light, keen April wind. The fisherman looked at him with the experienced compassion felt by the natives of the French Mediterranean coast for English visitors who bathe in the spring.

"It's nearly as cold as Brighton," Richie said, wrapping himself in his towel. "How are you, Barbary? And Raoul. I supposed you both at school this morning."

"Did you? We don't go there much now, as we're going away so soon. Are you going in now? "

"I certainly am. I want to put on a lot of warm clothes. And you? "

"No, we shan't be in till déjeuner. We aren't a great deal in the house. Just for meals and sleeping, usually. Though sometimes we sleep out. Do you do that in England much? "

"I don't. Some people in my college sleep in the garden when they think it's warm enough. I slept out too much in the war; I prefer a bed. . . . You won't be able to do it in London; I mean, there's nowhere to sleep."

Two pairs of melancholy and apprehensive eyes envisaged that remote wilderness of cold stone.

"I remember the river," said Barbary. "It was full of

31

ships and barges carrying wood and things. I got on a barge once and hid in a wood pile, and no one saw me till we were out to sea."

" I remember it. We were down at the wharfs together, and you sneaked away when I was talking to someone. I had to go to the police and set everyone searching, and when I got home without you there was the hell of a fuss. You were located that evening, and restored next day. I remember our parents discussing whether, for once in your life, they ought not to discard their humanitarian principles and do you physical violence. Father thought yes, and mother no; but as neither of them could or would wield a rod, I believe nothing came of it."

" No. But I was sent to bed at six for a week, with only bread and milk all day. That was daddy's idea. So mummy came up and amused me; she brought me marrons and candied fruit, and we played animal grab and piquet for pennies, only the pennies were all hers. And one evening, when daddy was out, I didn't go to bed; mummy and I drove round on the top of a bus, and had ices, and went to *Midsummer Night's Dream* in Regent's Park. And when we got back, daddy had come in, and he looked very cold at us—you know, with his eyebrows up, and not saying much. But I expect he said things to mummy after I'd gone to bed. . . . She never minded, did she ? "

" Never, that I know of. I believe she always did precisely what she liked."

Barbary was frowning, puzzled. " Yes. Then why . . ." Such a happy arrangement; why had it ever come to an end ? Richie perceived her drift, but did not follow it.

" The way you were reared, my child, explains why you are as we see you to-day. I remember often thinking how differently I should have been treated at school for conduct such as yours. So I have grown up a civilised being, and you, so far, have not. It is to be doubted if you ever will."

" Civilised . . ." Barbary seemed to examine civilisation, balancing it gravely, perhaps wistfully, against something else, and to reject it, as if it were mentioned too late.

She turned back to the sea's edge, where Raoul and the fisherman watched the fish in the net struggle, leap and die. Raoul went up the path to the Fraises.

* 3 *

A WEEK later Helen said good-bye to her son, her daughter and her stepson at the pink gate-posts of the Villa Fraises. She did not know when she would be seeing any of them again; Richie might come out for part of the long vacation; Barbary not so soon; Raoul perhaps never, since, when he returned to France, he would naturally go to his grand'mère in Bordeaux. His and Barbary's farewells to his friends had had the finality of permanent severance; they had themselves sounded that note, either from necessity or choice, regret or relief; perhaps they did not know which.

Raoul kissed his little stepbrother, and was kissed by his stepmother, looking pale and impassive, small and tidy in his going away clothes, the tears kept well back behind his eyes. Barbary's sallow olive face was clay-coloured as she clung to Roland so tightly that he squeaked; his fat arms hugged her close as he told her to come back quick; to put him from her was like dying.

She turned to her mother, and was lightly held for a moment in that cool embrace.

"Please write," she muttered, her voice strangling in her throat. "Oh, mummy, please write sometimes."

"Yes, I'll write," Helen assured her, and kissed her gently and without emphasis on her cold forehead.

"Oh, mummy . . . oh, mummy . . ."

The waiting fiacre was jingling its bells on the dusty road.

"It's time we started," Richie said.

Helen gently detached herself from her clinging child.

"Oh, mummy," whispered the strangling voice; "I can't bear it."

"Good-bye, my chicken. You'll be happy with your father."

"Mummy . . . *when*?"

"I can't say, bébé. It's not for ever, you know. You must make the best of it . . . and be good . . . as good as you can manage," she added, lightly qualifying an impossible admonition.

"Oh, mummy, I'm sorry." The choked whisper was less speech than a muted breath, shivering on the lemon-scented air; it did not reach Helen.

"Il faut nous dépêcher," the driver shouted. "Il faut partir."

They climbed into the fiacre; it jingled and clattered along the road, raising a whirl of white dust behind it.

Helen and Roland watched it out of sight, waving. Roland went on waving after it had disappeared round the first bend. "All gone," he shouted. "All gone away."

"Yes," she agreed. "All gone away."

"When Barby tummin back?"

"I don't know, darling."

He began to howl. "Want Barby, want Barby."

"Barby'll come back, my sweetie."

She took him down to the sea, to dig in the sand and forget. But still he would remark at intervals, "Want Barby," and she would soothe him with, "Barby coming soon." To herself she added, Want Maurice. Maurice is coming never; and turned from the sea that had swallowed Maurice up.

Her want of Maurice grew no less; it hungered in her night and day, engulfing her senses and her reason in an aching void. She tried to fill the void, stupefy the ache, with reading, translating, painting, gambling, chess, conversation with the abbé, games with Roland; but still it deepened about her, as if she were in a cave alone.

Coming in from the shore, she found that Lucien Michel, a cousin of Maurice's, who had sometimes stayed with them, had driven over from Toulouse and sat in the living-room. Helen was pleased to see him. He was an amusing, gay man of forty-five, and had a business in Toulouse; he and Maurice and she had had good times together in the past. She asked him to stay, which was what he had come to do. His company was both anodyne and stimulus, a stimulus she needed. She was one of the rare women who are almost as highly sexed as a man; yet she took sex casually in her stride; it was not an aim of existence, but a pleasure by the way, to be taken simply, directly, frankly, then laid aside for some other pleasure. She had been in love with her first husband and with her second; her grief for Maurice opened the door to any solace that came her way. Lucien admired her enormously, finding in her a woman's beauty and the mind, grasp and wit of a man. He guessed in her, too, a masculine freedom and sensuous-ness; most women, he held, loved not with their senses but with their sentiments. At the least, Helen was excellent company; at the best, she might be magnificent. He spent a week at the Fraises, and arranged to return for the next week-end.

* 4 *

A<small>T</small> Victoria the boat-train was met by a genial couple
who were Raoul's uncle and aunt. M. Armand Michel
was rather like his brother Maurice, and equally plump,
since the British way of life was no less nourishing than
that of a French collaborator. He received his nephew with
cordiality, though he thought he looked rather *triste*, like
his mother, a woman of little spirit. Barbary and Raoul
bade one another a casual good-bye and parted.

"Oncle Armand is like our stepfather," Richie said, as
they queued for a taxi; but Barbary said nothing to that.
Richie had observed that she did not care for their stepfather as a topic, and never pursued it; nor, for that matter,
did Raoul. It was as if Maurice, that genial collaborator,
of whom they had perhaps disapproved, had slipped out of
their memories when he was drowned in Collioure bay,
leaving a chill and haunting phantom in his place.

The house of Sir Gulliver Deniston was in the Adelphi;
it looked on the embankment gardens and the river with
an air of leisurely survival. Inside it Adam elegance was
enriched by a coloured Persian luxury which suggested the
island of Sybaris (influence of Helen), a chaste masculine
comfort (influence of Sir Gulliver), and a refurbishing of

gay cretonnes on cushions and curtains, with spring flowers
in jars (influence of Pamela). Sir Gulliver came out of his
library to welcome his children. He was distinguished
looking, pale, delicately featured, like Richie but better
looking; his eyes, rather penetrating than benevolent
behind their rimless pince-nez, seemed to withhold comment
on what he so keenly observed; he looked sceptical, ironic,
perhaps, like many lawyers, cynical; impatience was ridden
on a rein strong yet brittle; his temper, once roused, was
bitter and cold as ice.

Seeing his daughter Barbary standing before him, small
and slight in her travelling coat and crumpled frock, her
limp, hatless locks hanging round her pale, immature face,
her slate-grey eyes staring darkly up at him beneath black
brows, he did not see much change in her from the queer
elf of seven years ago. If he had supposed that the small
slattern of ten years old would have grown into a neat,
comely young creature of seventeen, who wore her clothes
well and waved her hair, he now perceived his error; he
saw before him the same little tramp; probably she still
hid on barges and rode on the bumpers of cars, seldom read
a book and never pushed a needle. Whatever her mother
and the lycée had taught her in these seven years, it had not
been to be a normal, nicely got up, pretty mannered girl.
Or so Sir Gulliver's experienced eyes, in one glance, summed
his daughter up. We shall see, he reflected, what Pamela
can do with her.

He kissed her with affection; she came from the enemy
camp, but none of it had been her fault. In the old days
she had been the pet of both parents, a harlequin, a vagrant

39

imp, who took her father amicably for granted, but would kiss her mother's shadow on the wall. Did she still feel like that? Helen's tremendous spell—perhaps no one ever quite escaped from it. Richie had not; he had not, for all his cold mortal anger, and for all his affection for the young Pamela.

"Well, Barbary." The pleasant voice that enticed and suggested the most improbable falsehoods from witnesses in court, and successfully wooed juries, sounded with its remembered timbre in her ears and brought childhood swinging back. "I'm very glad to see you. Did you have a good journey?"

"Yes, thank you."

Richie expanded and qualified this. The journey had been tolerable as journeys went, which, in 1946, was badly. The train had lost its way and wandered about the Hautes Pyrenées, till finally held up by a blocked line, arranged, the passengers had surmised, by the local maquis. Sir Gulliver inquired why. Richie explained that impeding trains was a maquis habit, contracted in the enterprising days of the Occupation, and now automatically continued; these Resisters still waged their war, resisting policemen, factories, rentiers, capitalists, collaborators, mayors and trains.

Sir Gulliver, having, with his experienced acceptance of strange forms of life, briefly considered these unfortunate automata, dismissed them as a topic.

His wife Pamela came down the stairs, with her year-old son in her arms; a handsome young woman of thirty, clear-skinned, brown-haired, athletically built, she looked

at once Amazonian and full of good sense. She welcomed
Barbary with breezy kindness, and introduced David.
Barbary, stabbed with thoughts of Roland, greeted him
with some constraint. She doesn't care for babies, Pamela
decided. So, tactfully, she changed the subject, talking
about Barbary's painting. She was to attend the Slade; it
was all arranged.

"If that's what you want to go in for," Sir Gulliver
said. "It will mean hard work, of course."

"How long for?" Barbary asked. "How long will I
be at the Slade?" It sounded long, not like the summer
holiday visit she had supposed.

"As long as you like," her father answered. "As long
as you find it of use. I was told that you would prefer it
to school."

"Yes. Besides, I go to school in France. . . ."

"You did, of course. You've left it now. A nearly
grown-up young woman."

She did not look that; more like a small trapped creature,
wary, apprehensive, turning her eyes from him to Pamela,
then to Richie, then to the floor.

"Do you want to come up to your room?" Pamela
asked her. "I expect you're pretty fagged."

Barbary followed her upstairs, and into a small bedroom
on the second floor, looking on the river.

"Richie said this was your old room." Pamela, her
baby in the crook of her arm, stood for a moment in the
doorway. Barbary looked round the room, walked to the
window, while the past came tumbling back at her,
a ghostly dream. The walls had been redistempered,

covering over the dado of pictures she had painted on
them, with her mother's help, when she had been nine and
ten. Her possessions had been tidied away: the teddy bear,
the dolls, the little tools with which she had made boats
and cut whistles, her old paint-box, her dolls' teaset. A
few old books were in the shelf by the window—*Masterman
Ready*, *The Little Duke*, *Coral Island*, *Black Beauty*, *The
Dog Crusoe*, *The Heroes*, *At the Back of the North Wind*.
All childish books; she had not been an advanced child;
nor was she yet; she would read all these again with
pleasure.

The bed had grown to full size; it was not the one in
which she had slept and woken, in which she had lain and
waited nightly for the step on the stairs, the tall figure
bending over her, the light caress followed by the close
embrace, the butterfly kisses from thick lashes moving
over her face, the tickling of the ribs bringing uncontrollable
giggles, the final cuddle and tucking in of bedclothes.
Sometimes after all this, to send her to sleep there would
be a few minutes of story telling: Perseus and Andromeda,
the Golden Fleece, Theseus and the Minotaur, something out
of Herodotus. One hand, or both, would be holding
tightly to the large cool hand that lay on the bed; the low,
trailing velvet voice, like rich cream, would flow on ... flow
into a dream.

Pamela had gone. Engulfed and assaulted by the re-
surrecting past, Barbary sat on the new bed, tears pricking
against her eyes; her face disintegrated into the quivering
chaos of sorrow. She fished for her handkerchief, grimy
from the train, and with it smudged back tears. They

welled up faster; giving in to them, she flung herself face downward on the bed and choked back sobs.

Someone presently knocked, waited a moment, said, "Can I come in?" and, as it was Richie, she said, "All right," and sat up, her back to the door.

"How are you getting on?" Richie asked. "Do you want a bath at once, or shall I have mine first?"

He paused a moment, then came farther in and shut the door.

"I'm afraid," he said, "this must all be pretty dim for you. London, I mean, after Collioure, and leaving mother and Roland and Raoul and all your friends, and not knowing anyone here except father and me, and scarcely remembering us. It must all feel pretty queer. But you'll go back sometime; and, after all, it's only fair that father should have his turn, after seven years. And you'll like him, he's fun, and lovely company. Though I admit that he takes some living up to, and rather keeps one on one's toes. If one mooches, seems stupid and dull, he gets bored. But not with you, he won't be. He likes daughters. And you'll get on all right with Pam, especially if you take to David. Then there'll be the Slade, and all London to see—pictures, and music, and ballet and buildings and plays. I should think it would be rather exciting, discovering London. You and I can do some sightseeing, till I go back to Cambridge. I don't really think, you know, it will be as bad as you feel it will be now."

Barbary had stopped sniffing. She spoke shakily.

"All right. But I don't mean to take any notice of David.

43

He's got no business here; nor has she. If they weren't here, mother could come back."

"Well," Richie said, "I don't think we can go into that. Mother doesn't want to come back, anyhow. And, if you want to get on with father, you'd better make friends with his wife and son. I find it easy enough to get on with Pam. She's not subtle, or exciting, but she's a good sort." His tone set the phrase fastidiously in quotation marks.

"She's no business here," Barbary repeated. "She oughtn't to *be* here."

"Oh, well." Richie waved this aside. "People do get about, you know. After all, father invited her. And I'm glad he did. She manages things very well for him; and he wouldn't want to live alone. I do trust, my dear, that you don't mean to sulk at Pamela."

"If she went away," Barbary speculated, "do you think mother would come back?"

"No. She went away before Pamela was there."

"Yes. But she went to France for a holiday, and then the war came. She would have come back. . . ." Her voice turned up in a dubious question.

"She could have, any time. She didn't want to." For the first time a touch of bitterness edged his negligent, easy tone. It occurred to Barbary that their mother had left Richie as well as their father; she alone had been taken, the chosen darling, who could never have been left.

"But *now*," she pressed it. "*Now* she would perhaps come back, if Pamela wasn't here. . . ."

"Oh, no," he returned. "No."

He looked back seven years into the past; knowing now

things of which, as a boy home for the holidays, he had
been only partly aware. He remembered incidents; dinner
parties for which guests arrived to find their hostess gone
out on her own occasions, or merely to evade the evening,
having decided that it would bore her. Arriving home
between ten and eleven, she would casually apologise—
Oh, I'm sorry, I couldn't get back, I do hope you had a
nice dinner. Sir Gulliver's brittle calm, his bland irony,
holding the social breakage lightly together, his witty talk
through the evening, till the last guests had gone; then his
icy, I hope you enjoyed your outing, and her unconcerned
response, yes, thank you, I really did. Though he did take
the first movement too fast . . . for she had been at a Queen's
Hall prom. Then, she went on, I met Eric, and we had
supper; I knew you would have finished dinner ages ago.
I hope the asparagus was nice, with that new sauce. Were
you bored, darling? There were several bores here; I don't
know how they get in to our house. Lady Elmslie, now . . .
Lord Elmslie had been a High Court judge; it was all a
pity. You had better go to bed, Richie. He had left them
to it, not deceived by his father's casual chilly lightness.
Did other people's mothers go on like this? He had feared
not; a fear that turned into resigned certainty as he grew
older.

Then there had been the long nights of cards, when his
mother had sat playing on and on, with a party of friends,
mostly men, enveloped in cigar smoke, knocking back
whisky, brandy, vodka, with enviable adult expertise (like
Mynheer Van Dunck. Helen never was drunk, but sipped
brandy and water gaily), acquiring and parting with piles

of chips that stood for incalculable wealth. Sometimes someone would drop out, declaring himself, in impenetrable society poker tones, to be finished. Helen had always played to the end; she might be finished financially, but never in spirit; she was like Charles Fox, her ancestor, who, having played and lost a fortune, would stake his gold watch, his horses, his houses, perhaps his mistresses. Would she, Richie wondered, have staked her children, if they had been of value to her fellow gamblers? Certainly she had once staked and lost her car. Sir Gulliver would, in the end go to bed; he had, he said, work to do next day. So upstairs he went; Richie, from his own room, would hear him enter his. Did he fall asleep, or would he lie awake wondering how much of his income was being played and lost below? Sometimes Helen won; she was a brilliant, if chancy, player; she won back the car; one night she won five hundred pounds, and with it bought the villa at St. Tropez to which she went with Barbary in 1939, the villa in which she had been living before the war broke, before she met Maurice. Had she meant to come back? Perhaps Sir Gulliver knew; no one else; he had always shut like a trap on his knowledge, on the whole affair of his wrecked marriage; Richie doubted if he even talked of it to Pamela.

"No," Richie said to Barbary. "I don't think she would ever come back. . . . Do you want a bath? No, I think I'll have mine first." He remembered that the hot water was limited, and suspected Barbary a reckless deep bather, used to the ocean.

Two minutes later someone else knocked. This time there

entered a rather broad woman of middle age; her face was plump, pleasant and pale, with long upper lip and wide, comfortable mouth. She said, in a slow, plump voice from Hampshire: " *Well*, Miss Barbary. Do you remember me, deary ? "

Barbary looked at her. The pleasant, broad face, the humorous mouth, came back to her across the gulf.

" *Coxy*," she said; for it was Mrs. Cox, the cook, who had been her friend seven years ago, who had fed her with tit-bits in the kitchen, whom she had loved.

" Coxy it is, bless your heart. And glad to see your face again in your own Pa's house, and more than time. And how's your Ma, love ? "

" Very well, thank you."

" Let me see—I don't rightly remember her name now. She married a French gentleman, didn't she ? "

" Yes. Her name is Michel."

" And I'm sure I hope she's happy with him, since it had to be."

" No, he died."

" There now, what a shame. Then your poor Ma's all alone now ? "

" She's got my little brother Roland."

At the mention of Roland, Barbary's voice quavered a little; it seemed to bring his darling shape so near.

" What, another baby, and a little Frenchman ? That's nice for her, isn't it ? I do miss your Ma. She made a lot of work, people coming about the house so much, and stopping up so late at night, and meals required at any time, and such a litter of cards everywhere, not to mention

47

your Ma's books and papers, and not much consideration shown, we used to think. But one thing I always said, your Ma was a true lady, being an Honourable and all that, and if she liked her fun she never interfered with ours; she let us have parties and our friends in, and never grudged. And she let us be; she was never one to be in and out of the kitchen, interfering about the meals and prying into the food. She employed me to furnish the meals, and furnish them I did, whoever did or did not eat them, for as to that we never knew what to expect. But she never niggled at the cost, or what might be or might not be left over, or what we was to have next day. She kept to her part of the house and we kept to ours. Unlike some."

Mrs. Cox darkly paused; then went on: "When your Pa was left all to himself, your dear Ma and you going off to France and then never coming back, I was that sorry for him, poor gentleman, left all alone but for Master Richie in the school holidays, and he was taken later, like all of them. I did my best for your poor Pa on the food we could get, and cooked very delicate and nice, the way he liked, and went shopping with the ration books and stood in the queues, and, 'Mrs. Cox,' he said, and more than once he said it, 'you make me very comfortable,' and so I ever tried to do. And then, without more than a bare word to me, having divorced your dear Ma, he went out and got married again and brought home his new young lady, which I don't wish to blame him for so doing, seeing as how your Ma had gone off with this French gentleman. But I would rather do for a single gentleman, they giving less trouble though eating more; and now I can't call my own kitchen my castle, for others intrude into it, giving orders and asking questions. And if your dear Ma was to walk in to-night and take her rightful place here, I won't say it wouldn't be a comfortable change."

"Oh, it *would*," Barbary breathed, clutching her damp handkerchief tightly in her hand. "It would be lovely, Coxy. Perhaps one day she will "

But Coxy looked dubious. "It would be very nice, love; but there would be awkwardness. Them that is here now would not go without a fight. And what your dear Pa would say, I don't know. . . . Never mind, ducks, you dry your eyes now and wash your face. And you come and talk to Coxy whenever you feel lonely. I remember as if it was yesterday your running into my kitchen wanting bread and jam to take out, or bread to throw to the birds, or eating the icing off my cakes as I made them. A proper little monkey you were, and running after your Ma as if you couldn't bear her out of your sight. And now here you are back in your own home, and your dear Ma's place filled by others. Well, life is a whirligig, and who knows what next? Now I must get back and see to my dinner. You and me'll have some nice talks later, about old times *and* new."

She went off; each had a warm sense of having found an ally against Others.

* 5 *

By the second week of May, Barbary was working at the Slade, where she went daily in a bus. The London streets all seemed to her very ugly and dull after Collioure. She lunched on sandwiches, and after the afternoon lessons often met Raoul, who attended a commercial school in Guilford Street, where he improved his English and learnt bookkeeping, accounts, shorthand and correspondence. They wandered about the dreary streets together, bought ices from barrows and any other food that seemed to them desirable, and often made their way down to the river, where they explored the wharfs and watched the barges. Urged by a desperate nostalgia, they could barely endure the meaningless grey city streets, the dull, respectable, smoke-dark houses. Nor did either of them desire to spend in their homes more time than they were obliged. Richie was back at Cambridge, Sir Gulliver a great deal in his chambers in the Temple; towards Pamela, Barbary felt hostile and shy.

" She's got into our house," she darkly told Raoul. " She has no business there; it's maman's house. She has a baby that sleeps in Roland's cot. Maman can't come home till she has gone."

" Will she go ? " Raoul inquired, as they sat together on a bus that careered along Holborn.

" No," said Barbary, morosely terse. " She won't. My father likes to have her in the house."

" One cannot blame him for that," Raoul kindly said. " They say that, without family life, old people go morally to pieces."

" And often, as to that, *with* family life," Barbary gloomily added.

They did not talk very much as a rule, as they went about together. Raoul would tell a little about his uncle and aunt; he liked his uncle, but as for his aunt, she did not want him about the house, there were too many children already; she preferred him to spend all day out. So, said Barbary, did the new wife of her father.

" My aunt says she's not the wife of your father, really, because he was divorced."

Barbary willingly accepted this view. " Then she's only his *chère amie*. And maman is still married to him, because her divorce didn't count either."

Raoul knew that; his aunt had more than once informed him that Barbary's maman had not been the wife of his papa.

" She ought to go," said Barbary, still brooding over her stepmother. " As they're not married. However, married or not, she's there. I mean to be a great deal out of the house. I've found a place; I'll show you. We get off in Cheapside."

They got off in Cheapside, and walked up Foster Lane. Having crossed Gresham Street, the road became a lane

51

across a wrecked and flowering wilderness, and was called Noble Street. Beyond Silver Street, it was a still smaller path, leading over still wilder ruins and thicker jungles of greenery, till it came out by the shell of a large church.

" You see," said Barbary nonchalantly, " there are lots of empty houses and flats."

Raoul saw that this was so. Neither he nor Barbary was surprised, or even greatly interested; these broken habitations, this stony rubbish, seemed natural to them.

" And nice gardens." Barbary, with an estate agent's smug and optimistic manner, indicated the forest of shrubs and flowers and green creeping things running about the broken city in the evening sunshine. They were in a strip of green beside the church; elder tree boughs crowded into a gaping west window; tall weeds waved about tombstones. They sat on a large flat stone, whereunder lay Sir William Staines, Mrs. Alice Staines, and their large family of children, who had left, about two centuries ago, an only and affectionate sister to lament their loss.

" I've taken a house here," said Barbary. " It's called Somerset Chambers. It's between the church and the café."

She led the way into Fore Street, where what was left of Somerset Chambers gaped on the street. They climbed a steep, winding flight of stone stairs, past lavatories, past rooms with walls and fireplaces patterned in green and yellow tiles, and panelled doors lying on the littered floors. Here lived, according to an inscription on the staircase wall, the Brenner Brothers, Ltd.; their names were Joseph and Emil.

" It's an office," Barbary explained. " They don't live here."

They climbed higher, past another lavatory; the stairs spiralled up, fouled by pigeons, ending abruptly in a boarded roof.

" Look, we can climb through it," said Raoul, pleased.

Barbary nodded. In the boards there was a gap large enough to squeeze through; they did so, and stood, with no roof but the sky, while pigeons whirred about them and the wind blew in their faces, on a small plateau, looking down over the wrecked city.

Suddenly the bells of St. Paul's clashed out, drowning them in sweet, hoarse, rocking clamour. Barbary began to dance, her dark hair flapping in the breeze as she spun about. Raoul joined her; they took hands, snapping the fingers of the other hand above their heads; it was a dance of Provence, and they sang a Collioure fisherman's song in time to it.

The bells stopped. The children stood still, gazing down on a wilderness of little streets, caves and cellars, the foundations of a wrecked merchant city, grown over by green and golden fennel and ragwort, coltsfoot, purple loosestrife, rosebay willow herb, bracken, bramble and tall nettles, among which rabbits burrowed and wild cats crept and hens laid eggs.

" I shall perhaps keep a hen," Barbary said. " Or perhaps we can find the eggs of the wild hens. And look, there are plenty of fig-trees. We can cook meals in the flat, or perhaps in that big café next door. We must bring rugs to sleep on, and any food we can get from home."

Raoul looked dubious about this. " My aunt wouldn't
let me. And she keeps the food locked up."

" We'll buy some. Do you know what I'm going to do ?
Paint views on postcards and sell them in the street. I shall
sit in our flat and paint. I shall spend the afternoons here
instead of at the Slade. You can come on from school.
It's best in the evenings, and on Saturdays and Sundays,
because no workmen are about then. The Brenners aren't
here either, nor any of the other people."

" How do you know," Raoul inquired, when they were
down on the first floor again, " that this flat is not already
occupied ? "

" It hasn't that air. Anyhow, it is ours now, and I shall
write our names on the walls."

" There are a number of names on the walls of the
lavatories. And drawings too."

" That means nothing. Lavatories are like that: people
like to write and draw on the walls."

This familiar law of nature was known also to Raoul;
it obtained in Collioure as well as elsewhere.

" But," said Barbary, " I shall paint our names on the
walls of the staircase too, like the Brenner brothers. Then
the flat will be known for ours. If anyone comes round
for rent, I shall pay it. My father gives me money."

" My uncle only a very little." Raoul reflected sadly on
the difference in the financial habits of English lawyers and
French merchants, which seemed to him considerable.

" Let's go out on the terrace," said Barbary.

From the stairs a great gap in the wall opened on to an

earthy lead terrace, grown with dandelions and yawning with holes.

"Look. We can look from here into the church."

They peered down through the great broken circle of what had been the east window; below it the altar had stood; they looked along the bare nave to the tower end, where, in the west window, ragged painted glass swung muttering in the wind. Above the pointed arches of the clustered columns of the aisles, which still stood, angels' heads serenely gazed at emptiness. To the walls a few niches clung, where monuments of the dead had once been; grass and marigolds grew over them in tufts.

"Is it Catholic?" Raoul asked.

"I shouldn't think so. Most churches here aren't."

They re-entered Somerset Chambers and went downstairs, coming out into Fore Street. Next door was the Zita Café, open to the street, a large room, empty but for rubble. Outside it was painted its name, and inside " Snacks and Light Refreshments. Accommodation for 60 Persons. Large Dining-room Downstairs." Above this notice was a landscape painting on the wall, a road running through fields. Downstairs was the dining-room, the grill, the kitchen with its range. It had been a very fine café.

"We can eat here," they said. "Downstairs, where it will be more private. We can make a fire and cook."

They went round outside the church. On the front porch a notice said " The Church is open for Private Prayer and Devotion every Week Day from 10 a.m. till 4 p.m. Saturdays 10 a.m. till 1 p.m. Entrance in Fore Street." The door was locked. From the green garden of weeds

55

and gravestones outside the west wall, they scrambled on
to a window ledge and dropped down inside the church.
It was windy and bare; the iron spokes and wire gauze in
the empty windows flapped to and fro. They went into
the belfry tower; eight great bronze bells lay broken on
the floor, by a bronze statue of a man with long hair and
high boots. Torn fragments of hymn-books littered the
floor. A narrow stairway spiralled up the tower.

"Pigeons," said Raoul, peering up it. "Why do pigeons
make stairs always their lavatory?"

Barbary was looking at the bells.

"One could hide in them, if one could tip them up and
get under them. But they are too heavy."

"But two lie on their sides," said Raoul. "We could
get into those."

They did so, curling up small. It was their maquis
training; they had learnt to look for and find cover
everywhere.

They climbed out through the window, and made their
way about the ruined, jungled waste, walking along broken
lines of wall, diving into the cellars and caves of the underground city, where opulent merchants had once stored
their wine, where gaily tiled rooms opened into one
another and burrowed under great eaves of overhanging
earth, where fosses and ditches ran, bright with marigolds
and choked with thistles, through one-time halls of
commerce, and yellow ragwort waved its gaudy banners
over the ruin of defeated business men. The shells of
churches and wrecked guild halls stood thickly on the
ground. Until you looked and saw that they were shells,

you would have supposed the churches to be going concerns, for they bore such legends as " Divine Service. Sundays, Holy Communion 11. Evensong 6. Open daily for Private Prayer, Rest and Meditation. A Hearty Welcome to All." Some, however, less diehard, admitted that the congregation now worshipped in some other church.

" My uncle and aunt," said Raoul, " go to church. My aunt is devout. I have to go, too, on Sundays and saints' days, though I told them I was anti-clerical and never went at home."

" My father's woman goes to church too. She goes to a lawyers' temple. She tried to make me go too; she says the lawyers take turns at reading the Bible aloud there, and last Sunday it was my father's turn. But I don't think she really much wanted me to go. Richie says he is High Church, but I don't know what that means. He may turn Catholic, he says, one day, but hasn't made up his mind. If *I* went to church, I should go to one of these."

" Me too," Raoul agreed. They surveyed the gaping shells, the tall towers, the broken windows into which greenery sprawled, the haunted, brittle beauty, so forlorn and lost in the wild forsaken secrecy of this maquis: it was their spiritual home.

" I shall go to the one next our flat," said Barbary. " I like it."

" No priests." Raoul, anti-clerical, approved of this.

" I shall preach," Barbary said.

" No pulpit."

" I shall preach from that window we looked through

57

from the terrace. Or else from one of the niches on the walls."

" What shall you say ? "

Barbary considered. " I shall say how divorced people can't really marry again. And I shall preach about hell, like Père Richaud at the Lycée. They don't have much hell in the English Church, Richie says. But we'll have hell in our church."

" If there is anything, there must be hell," Raoul remarked, reasonable and matter of fact. " But one supposes that there is nothing."

" It is a pity," Barbary said, after a moment, " that if we others do wicked things, they stay done. Christians can undo what they've done by confession and absolution. Do you remember Henri Leclos at Port Vendres, him who attacked little girls ? Then one day he was nearly drowned in a storm and he repented and got absolution and began a new life. So it was all right for him, but it made no difference to the little girls and their parents. If you are a Christian, you just think how you have sinned against God, and God will forgive you if you repent. But we others can't be forgiven, because we sin only against people, and the people stay hurt or killed, or whatever it is we have done to them. It would be better to be a Christian and get forgiveness, and only mind about God and hell. Perhaps I shall myself turn devout, in that church."

" It is not a Catholic church." Raoul, though he shared with most of his maquis friends a distaste for Roman Catholic churches, could only with difficulty entertain the idea that there were others.

"That does not matter," Barbary, broader minded, told him, "since I am not a Catholic."

They emerged from the fantastic ruined city into Cheapside.

"It is formidable, how London is ugly," Raoul commented, looking with melancholy disgust at the noisy street and grey Victorian houses.

"St. Paul's is not," Barbary said. "That great dome, and the columns, and the high steps up. To-morrow afternoon is Saturday, and I shall go to our flat and clean it a little, and perhaps paint a picture. I shall bring a cushion to sit on, and some food. You come any time you like, and bring anything you can to eat. But I can bring some for you too. Coxy lets me have anything I want. She is the great comfort of my life."

* 6 *

DINNER had begun; the Denistons had friends. Barbary, having cursorily washed some of the dirt of ruined London off her hands, but not changed either frock or shoes, slipped into the dining-room and into her place at the table. What a mess, the others thought, she was in; the two guests concealed surprise. Sir Gulliver and his wife felt none; nevertheless, Sir Gulliver raised his eyebrows a little.

" May one ask what branch of art you have been practising this evening? Drawing in charcoal? "

" No. Just in pencil." Barbary glanced down at the front of her frock, perceiving it to be smudged and smeared with the earth and dust of Somerset Chambers and its parish church.

" I'm sorry," she added, " I didn't have time to change."

" Pray," said her father politely, " don't mind us. Artists are proverbially Bohemian."

After dinner Barbary, who did not care for visitors, went out and walked on the embankment, looking at the shining river lapping against the wall and the steamers hooting past. A man spoke to her as she leant over the wall.

" Nice evening."

" Yes, it is."

" Going anywhere, ducks? "

" No."

" What about if you and me had a stroll? "

" No, thank you, I'm going home now. Good night."

" Good night, proudy." He moved away, to pick up a more companionable girl.

Barbary wondered what the ruined waste lands looked like after dark, with the night lying over the deep chasms, the pits, the broken walls and foundations, the tangled greenery, the roofless, gaping churches, the stone flights of stairs climbing high into emptiness, the hidden creatures scrambling and scuttering among brambles. Strange it would be, and frightening, the lost waste maquis in the dark, haunted by who knew what of wandering, sinister, lurking things of night. For it was there, surely, that such beings would foregather, as they had foregathered in the Forêt behind Collioure, the uneasy fringe that hung about the Resistance, committed by their pasts to desperate deeds. Where should the London Resistance movement have its headquarters but among the broken alleys and caves of that wrecked waste? It had familiarity, as of a place long known; it had the clear, dark logic of a dream; it made a lunatic sense, as the unshattered streets and squares did not; it was the country that one's soul recognised and knew.

Barbary let herself into the house; the visitors had just gone. She met Pamela in the hall.

" Really, Barbary. Don't you think you are rather *too* casual and extraordinary? "

" Am I? "

61

"Coming in late to dinner all over dirt, and in those filthy canvas shoes, then disappearing and going out by yourself. . . . You do behave in the oddest way, I must say. I mean, I know you grew up abroad, and all that . . . but I could see the Akensides thought it pretty queer."

"Well, I was late, and if I'd changed I'd have been later still. And the Ake—whatever they are—didn't want to talk to *me*. So I went out."

"Your father wasn't awfully pleased, you know. I expect he'll tell you. After all you *are* living in his house. Richie never goes on like that when he's at home; he's always so polite to people. I really do think you might try a little."

Sir Gulliver came in; he had been seeing the Akensides to Charing Cross underground station.

"So," he observed to Barbary, "you have reappeared. I take it you have been out."

"Yes. On the embankment."

He looked at her speculatively, as if he were considering how much it might be worth while to say to so untaught a young creature, brought up in so negligent a way.

"I am not, I hope, a prude," he suavely remarked; "but at your age it is perhaps on the whole better not to make a habit of wandering alone on the embankment after dark. There are some queer people about in this part of London, who might misunderstand your aims and annoy you. Speak to you, I mean. It might be tiresome for you."

"I don't mind. They go away if you say you don't want them."

Her father exchanged looks with his wife, whose resigned

shake of the head expressed, I wash my hands of this; it is beyond me, and your affair.

He said, more nearly sharp than usual, "Don't be childish, my dear Barbary. There are ways of behaviour that you must really learn. Possibly I ought to have sent you away to school, where you would have learnt them. As it is, you must take them from me, and from Pamela, and try to become a normally civilised young woman. Those shoes, for example. . . . Now, I think it's time you went to bed. Good night."

They kissed one another, with distance. The kissing habit had not, between Barbary and Pamela, developed, since neither desired it.

In their bedroom Sir Gulliver and his wife discussed his daughter.

"I presume," he commented, "that she will learn how to behave in time. You must do your best with her."

"I'm afraid," said Pamela, "that she'll learn nothing from me. She seems to resent my being here. I dare say it's natural, but it doesn't make life any easier."

"Resents it?" He frowned at the word. "What right . . . Oh, well . . ."

He pondered over it for a moment.

"As a child," he said, "she was wholly wrapped up in her mother. I can't make out if she still is. I can't get her to mention her. And, as I find it difficult to mention her myself, the subject isn't mooted. I don't even know if she writes; nor how she feels about the whole situation. Nor do I know what she has been told about the past; what light she sees me in: I dare say a poor one."

" She sometimes gets letters from France. But I doubt if she writes any. I think she only draws pictures on postcards and posts them to her little stepbrother."

" Ah, yes. Richie told me she was quite devoted to the child."

" The Akensides," said Pamela, after a moment, " are sending Ruth to Downe. She's getting rather out of hand at home, Mrs. Akenside says."

What they both thought was, if Barbary were a year or two younger she, too, might have been sent to Downe. What Pamela also thought was that they had now talked about Barbary enough.

* 7 *

FRAGMENTS of hymn-books, torn and charred, were scattered about the church and belfry floor. Out of one of the cracked bronze bells lying on their sides Barbary picked a grimy clump of pages, spread open at the Dies Irae. "Day of wrath," she read aloud, " O day of mourning! See fulfilled the prophet's warning, Heaven and earth in ashes burning! Oh what fear man's bosom rendeth when from Heaven the Judge descendeth. . . ."

It reminded her of Père Richaud and his sermons about hell. The tune was scored above the words. Walking up the aisle, as if in procession, Barbary sang it to herself and Raoul.

> " When the wicked are confounded,
> Doomed to flames of woe unbounded,
> Call me with Thy Saints surrounded. . . .
>
> " Ah, that day of tears and mourning!
> From the dust of earth returning,
> Man for judgment must prepare him;
> Spare, O God, in mercy spare him! "

Reaching the east end of the chancel, she bowed three

times, then knelt and struck her breast, as they did in the
Collioure church.

"Raoul!" she called. "Come and repent. With Thy
favoured sheep O place me, Nor among the goats abase me.
Raoul, you must repent, so that you don't go to hell.
You can repent, because you were brought up a Catholic.
I can't, because I'm a heretic, and heretics can't undo what
they've done."

"I shan't repent by myself," Raoul answered. He was
climbing about the corrugated iron and tarpaulin that
roofed the crypt. Through the empty window-frames
green boughs thrust; the iron spokes swung teetering and
creaking in the breeze, like the broken signs of inns.

Barbary climbed up into an empty niche in the wall,
where the bust of John Speed had once stood. She began
to preach in French about hell fire, imitating the accent
and gestures and ejaculations of the good Père Richaud.
In her vehemence she overbalanced, and fell out of the
niche on to the floor, bruising her knee.

"That is what you get," Raoul told her, "for preaching
of hell. I would rather hear no more of hell. It is not our
affair."

They strolled about the church, and into the belfry
tower where the bronze statue of the poet stood, but they
did not know him for a poet, they supposed him a British
clergyman. They climbed the pigeon-fouled steps up the
tower, as far as they could get, and down into the church
again.

"Now we'll have supper in the café," said Barbary.
They went there, and down the steps where the notice said

"Large Dining-room downstairs." They sat on a brick ledge in the ruined dining-room, and fished out of Barbary's basket sandwiches of ham and liver paste and slices of bread and margarine and bottles of lemonade and some buns, and began to eat and drink.

"I expect," said Raoul, "some of them will soon arrive."

"They are sure to," said Barbary.

Before the meal was finished they did so; two young men and a girl, coming quietly down the stairs, the men in rubber shoes and clothes that seemed to have come together haphazard, the girl smart, scarlet lipped and nailed, with a mane of waved fair hair; she looked good humoured and common, her companions furtive and shabby. One of them was auburn haired, delicate featured, freckled; the other dark, good looking, and astute; they were, respectively, Glasgow Irish and Isle of Dogs; the girl was from Bankside, and had worked as a messenger in the city until her place of business had gone up in flames. She knew the ruins intimately, calling them and the anonymous alleys that ran between them by their old names, peopling them with industrious business men, chattering, tea-bibulous typists, messengers and clerks: she moved among ghosts, herself solid, cheerful and unconcerned. She had done no regular work since that fatal night when the city had blazed; she lived randomly, now helping her mother with the wharfside pub, now straying the streets; her name was Mavis.

"Hallo, kids." The greeting was Mavis's; the young men, more wary, glanced round the large dining-room,

looking into its shadowy corners and recesses, as if someone
might lurk there.

Reassured, they took seats, producing the sandwiches,
bottles of beer, and other delicacies which Mavis had
kindly brought them from her mother's pub, and affably
remarking, " Hiya, chickens."

" Quite well, thank you," they replied. Barbary added:
" I brought some extra food, in case anyone who came
hadn't enough."

" That's right," said the dark young man, who was called
Horace (surnames were taboo; it was bad form, and also
useless, to inquire into them). " There's never enough."

Mavis told him he was a one; she loved him dearly.
He was a wharf rat, and his intimate knowledge of the
waterside matched hers of the city. Only Jock from
Glasgow knew little of London; he had a kind of cunning
lost innocence that linked him with the two young creatures
from France. To these two, their companions and all those
others who from time to time haunted the ruins were the
maquis, the Resistance, their hands against the police and
the powers that ruled, their aim to rob society of the
livelihood they required and had somehow forfeited. The
children of the French maquis knew their own kind. The
London maquis thought them very rum, but were too
polite to inquire what they had done, or what was the
cause of the police-phobia they evinced. Not that police-
phobia, that natural and laudable distaste of the properly
constituted human mind, required much cause. But,
whereas all that the Londoners desired regarding the police
force was that they should succeed in keeping out of its

way, the kids from abroad seemed inspired with a lively animosity that caused them to be at pains to think up such methods of annoyance and outrage as they could perpetrate with reasonable safety. Though the Londoners disliked policemen, and more particularly military policemen, they did not look on them with the grim and righteous disapproval that scowled from the faces of Barbary and Raoul at the sight of a blue helmet.

Horace produced from his pockets a bundle of ration books, which he reflectively examined.

" Good for a few days," he said. " Till the beggers stop them. They don't remember to do it at once, they're too busy searching. After that it's a bit of a risk. You can usually get away with the points and the tea and the sweets, though."

" Any clothes kewps? " Mavis asked.

" Not for you, gorgeous." Horace repocketed a little red book. " The rate in the pubs on my beat has gone up to half a crown a kewp."

" Have a heart. I'll give you five bob for three. I need stockings."

" What a girl! If you can't liberate a pair, you're not worth helping. I thought it was your job to help us poor beggers, not us you."

" Well, I do help you, don't I? I got you a lovely ration book last week. But I don't have to. There's other boys after me, you know."

" Dessay. You'd better watch your step. You know what you get from me when I catch you at tricks. A sound spanking. You're mine, and don't you forget it."

Mavis's blue eyes looked at him sidelong from under their messy black lashes. Beneath her maidenly efforts to conceal with bantering insults her grovelling devotion, she was Horace's slave, and both knew it. Had he looked at Barbary (who was not at all his type) with the affectionate eyes which Glasgow Jock turned on her, she would have made a scene.

Horace got up. " I'm off. Coming, Mave? "

They strolled away together, along Fore Street, past what had been Barclay's Bank, and through what had been St. Giles's rectory garden, between the Jews' burying ground, built over after the Jews were banished with fair summer-houses for pleasure, later with warehouses for Jews returned. They passed, without knowing it, Mayor Richard Whittington's spring of clear water near the parsonage, and the house and almshouses of the brotherhood of St. Giles's, but Mavis only remembered there a house of Japanese merchants and other houses of other merchants who had manufactured clothes, typewriters, imitation jewellery, umbrellas. They skirted a massive bastion of wall, broken, tree-grown, assaulted by casualty of war, and later by that of demolition men; crossing Barbers' Hall, that gaping chasm where fireweed ran over Inigo Jones's court-room, they entered the tiny path of Monkwell Street, where once the Abbot of Clarendon's monks had lived and owned a well; where later residents had lived and manufactured and imported and sold; Mavis remembered them all, those vanished houses of commerce where now the jungle sprawled.

" I left some cigarettes for you at Johnson and Brown's," said Mavis. " May's well call for them."

The offices of Messrs. Johnson and Brown, tailors, were at the corner where Monkwell Street curved into Noble Street at Falcon Square. Into their wild caves Horace and Mavis dived among bracken and bramble, starting a rat as they entered. Behind a screen of deep shrubbery lay packets wrapped in torn fragments of mackintosh— cigarettes, sweets, ration books, watches, fountain pens; the hard-won miscellaneous fruits of quick wits, quick hands, and ruthless purpose. Among them Horace and Mavis lay on rugs filched from cars; love passed between them, and clothing coupons, as was right in a tailor's shop.

They sat, though they did not know it, and nor had Messrs. Johnson and Brown, and nor did anyone in that year of 1946, in the garden of a great house of stone and timber anciently belonging to the Nevilles; a great gabled house over against a bastion of the Wall, perished nearly three centuries since in another great fire. If ghosts walked in that garden plot, they were ghosts of good family, but friendly to tailors, for in their day the nobility did not scorn commerce. They might, however, have scorned the two untutored pilferers who sat now in their ancient domains among stolen goods.

" I am very, very fond of ruins, ruins I love to scan," Mavis hummed. She pointed across the wilderness towards the bastion. " That's Mr. Monty's room up there, that was. Mr. Monty always had his joke. He'd look in at the warehouse—that was our warehouse, that pit with the pink flowers and nettles all over it—pretty, isn't it? Mr. Monty'd

71

look in and speak to old Mr. Dukes, he was the head clerk, and he'd have his joke with him, except on a Monday morning, and then it was look out for squalls. Poor Mr. Dukes, he was ever so upset when it all went; for weeks he'd go wandering about the ruins, seeing if he could save anything, but of course he couldn't, what the fire left the rescue men grabbed as quick as you could say knife."

Horace looked wistful; but for that blasted army, he too might have been a rescue man, hurrying to incidents, working away in dungarees with great deep pockets. When he had escaped from the army, incidents had been over, but for a few V 2s, and, anyhow, to join Civil Defence would have been to make himself much too noticeable. Life was bitterly unfair.

" Those kids," he said presently. " I don't get it. What do you think? Are they on the up and up? Do they know we're on the run? They could put us away easy."

" Not them. They don't know a thing; they're too dumb, anyhow, and they hate the cops like hell. They call them the Gestapo, and want to go gunning for them. If you ask me, they're nuts. But harmless . . . Jock's getting soft on the girl."

" I suppose he'll get talking to her, the silly sod. He can't mind his tongue. He'll let out his name, I wouldn't wonder. He's no more sense than a kid. I dunno why I stick with him."

" Oh, Jock's all right." Mavis, in the lazy content of love, did not care who told anybody what; there was always a way out of a jam, and Horace always found it; Horace was clever.

" Look, Horace: if you do get copped one day, either
for you know what or for anything else, you might get to
a lovely prison my Uncle Bert's staying at. There was a
piece about it somewhere. They call it a free prison—
Leyhill or somewhere. They have a lovely time, no locked
doors, and they could all get away, but no one wants to,
it's so comfortable. And the food's something lovely. They
go out driving tractors, or whatever they like, and have
real good evenings when they get back ; Uncle Bert says
there's darts and billiards and the wireless on; there's one
room where they have that awful Third Programme on,
I suppose that's a punishment cell. Uncle Bert's sore on
account he'll soon be out; he says he means to get back
there as soon as ever he can, it's much comfier than anything
outside."

" *I'd* never make it," Horace gloomily said. " You bet
they'd put me in a bug-house and starve me, if once they
got their hands on me."

In the café the other three still sat, talking about life and
housing and such matters.

" There's a nice high stair at 13 and 14 Addle Street,"
Raoul said. " At the top there is a room, and all up the
stairs are toilettes, and a toilette also at the top. The
merchants must have spent much time in toilettes. I think
perhaps it is nicer there than in Somerset Chambers."

" You go there, then, son," Jock suggested.

" No, I will now go home. My uncle and aunt become
severe when I am late, and too, I have to do my home
work."

He slipped away into the ruinous twilight, treading

lightly along broken walls above shadowed chasms and catacombs. Evening darkened over that lost waste, where merchants and lawyers, clerks, typists, shopkeepers, tailors and chemists had their deserted lairs, now the dens of wolves and wild cats. A fine maquis, Raoul thought, in which to lurk and plot and hide from the Gestapo, lying in wait for them, tripping them up into brambled ravines, shooting at them from behind broken walls.

A cat—or was it a wolf?—leaped from beneath his feet and fled scuttering among rocks. He started, and hurried on, running down Monkwell Street, past Barbers' Hall, past the Coopers' Arms at the corner of Silver Street, past St. Olave's churchyard, past all the ruined halls, down the narrow alley of Noble Street that cut across the jungle to Gresham Street, past the church of St. Anne and St. Agnes with its gardens full of fig-trees, and the churchyard of St. John Zachary, bright with dahlias and sunflowers, and so down Foster Lane into Cheapside, where streets were paved and buildings stood up, and a solid, improbable world began, less real, less natural than the waste land.

" SHALL you and me go up into Somerset and bide quiet a wee while? " Jock said softly to Barbary. Barbary considered him with experienced eyes.

" You'd want to do that stupid thing."

" 'Tisn't stupid . . . I wouldn't do a thing you don't want. . . . But don't you like me a wee bit, then? "

" I like you very much. But I don't like that thing men want to do. I don't see why anyone likes it; it's no fun."

" It is that, when two feel love. It's only natural."

" I suppose it must be, as people and animals all seem to do it. But I can't see why because you love someone you want to do that. I mean, what has it to do with loving? I wonder who thought of it first."

" Adam and Eve in the garden," said Jock, a well-brought-up Catholic youth.

" Oh, yes. Père Richaud was always talking about them. Well, I suppose they liked it. I don't see anything in it; it seems just silly and uncomfortable. Let's talk instead. Tell me about some of the things you've done, and why you're hiding and can't have your own ration book. Have you killed people? "

" Only Jerries in France, darlin'. And not many of them ones either. I don't like killing, an' that's a fact."

" Well then, what *have* you done? "

" Ah, I can't tell you. But I'm on the run, and so's Horace, and so are hundreds like us, and all through no fault of ours. The law's an awfu' cruel thing when it's after huntin' men down that've done no wrong to any."

" How long must you hide? "

" There's none knows that. Maybe months, maybe years, maybe for always. We change our names and make new beginnings, but not God nor all His saints can give us true identity cards and ration books of our own. So we have to take them where we can, and make a wee bit of money too to put sup and drink in our bellies. I've been a casual down at the docks on and off this last month. But a man gets awfu' tired of liftin' and carryin'. And forbye, with the police snooping round, it's no safe. I'd sooner do canny jobs on the side. . . . Look, lassie, I've something for you."

He pulled a soft brown leather wallet from his coat pocket; in it was a powder case and puff, a lipstick and a bottle of scent.

" I've saved it for you," he explained. " I got it last night in Jermyn Street."

" It's nice." Barbary fingered the soft leather. " I can keep my paints in it. You took it from someone, didn't you? "

" Ah." Jock looked smug. " So what about a kiss now? "

" All right. Only not the other thing—no, I won't, I

hate it." She struggled free, leaving him cross but resigned.

" You're a queer lassie. Did you never, then ? "

She was silent; she would not tell him. A thin, fair young face, the face of the enemy, the harsh, broken French of the conqueror, the smell of the forest in October, of wild apples and wood fires and heath . . . later the maquis had killed him.

" I've done with all that," she said.

No one had known. They knew that she had been caught by the Germans, beaten a little, released with a warning. They did not know that she had met again in the forest the one who had ordered her to be beaten and released; met him three times, and the third time it was a trap. They had only known of the trap, and had praised her for her cunning.

" I'm going home now," said Barbary.

They walked together through the wilderness, past the gaping shells of churches.

" Do you go to church, Jock ? " she asked him absently.

" Not me," he said. " Not now. . . . Mind you, I can go when I've a mind to. I don't need to die in sin."

" No, I suppose not. I suppose you've done terrible sins, Jock."

" No worse than others. I can repent when I've a mind, and then I'll be in the clear. There's always forgiveness waitin'; God's not like the law, to destroy a man that confesses."

" So then it's all right again. But that's only for Catholics, isn't it ? "

" Everyone should be Catholic. . . . Mind now . . ."

He caught hold of her; the path they walked had broken into a deep chasm; it yawned darkly before them, a pit into which unbelievers fell and lay without hope, among sprawling weeds and dead creatures, as in a shambles of slain beasts of the chase painted by Jean-Baptiste Oudry.

" But I don't see," Barbary pursued her thoughts, " that it undoes what you've done."

"What doesn't? " They were threading their way down the broken wall and up the other side of the abyss.

" Repenting and confessing. It only puts *you* right, not what you've done to people."

" It'll keep you from hell. Isn't that enough now? . . . You're the queer lassie, to be talkin' about them things when you're out with a lad. If you want to know about religion, you should find a priest and ask him will he give you instruction."

" No. I know about it."

"Well, will you be this way to-morrow? "

" Yes. Sunday morning. I shall paint postcards. Good night, Jock."

" Give us a kiss, then."

They embraced and parted. He was a gentle and reasonable youth; he was fond of her without much passion, desired her, but not more than his system could easily sustain, and her aloof, childish uncomprehension cooled his blood. He supposed her very backward, since she failed to see the most obvious connection in the world. He had before encountered young female creatures to whom this connection was puzzling and obscure; but they had grasped it in the end, and so, no doubt, would Barbary.

* 9 *

SUMMER slipped on ; a few blazing days, when London and its deserts burned beneath a golden sun, and the flowering weeds and green bracken hummed with insects, and the deep underground cells were cool like churches, and the long dry grass wilted, drooped, and turned to hay; then a number of cool wet days, when the wilderness was sodden and wet and smelt of decay, and the paths ran like streams, and the ravines were deep in dripping greenery that grew high and rank, running over the ruins as the jungle runs over Maya temples, hiding them from prying eyes.

Barbary, leaving the Slade at noon, would stroll about the ruins, painting and selling postcards to American tourists and others; she and Raoul became familiar figures in that fantastic landscape. With the money thus earned they would amuse themselves about London, buy food and cigarettes for themselves and their fellow maquisards, hiding the packets in caves and holes and in the high chambers that reared against the sky at the top of winding stone stairways. Sometimes the packets were taken; there were many prowlers by night who frequented the maquis; some Barbary and Raoul got to know, others not. All, known and unknown, they regarded as Resistance workers, to be supported and helped. Resistance against what and whom, Mavis once asked them. Against, Raoul replied, the Gestapo, the Fascists, the laws ; and Horace said, " That's right, son. Throw in the army as well and you've said it."

" The army, it is Fascist ? " Raoul supposed.

" Fascist ? Jesus, it's Nazi, it's worse than Hitler and the Gestapo and the Jerries and the Eyeties all put together. No one's free to eat or breathe or live, with that damned army about the place. Let's see, what are those four footling freedoms we used to hear about—freedom to eat, freedom to speak, freedom to get about—what's the other ? Freedom from fear, that's it. Well, who's going to have freedom from fear with those bleeding M.P.s snooping round after him ? "

" That's silly, freedom from fear," Mavis, a sensible girl, remarked. " Who's ever going to have that ? And any-one that did would soon come to a sticky end, dashing into the traffic regardless, and getting into fields with bulls."

" Freedom from fear of the policeman knocking at the door, I've heard say it means," Jock dubiously said. " And we ought to have it, it's our right. But we have no such thing at all. What call have policemen to be knocking on our doors at all hours, putting fear into us ? I've heard say it should only be the postman and the milkman that knocks, and so it should. Wasn't it Churchill said that, or one o' them big shots ? Then why don't they stop 'em from knocking, that's what I'm asking ? "

They brooded over this conundrum in melancholy disgust.

"Oh, I've *had* them," Horace angrily dismissed the police, the army, the four freedoms, and the big shots that shot their mouths off. "What's the sense in anything? It's each for himself and grab what you can, and lucky if you keep alive."

"Et merde au Gestapo," Raoul added, his mournful eyes on his bruised knuckles, for at school that morning he had come to blows with someone who had told him that the French had licked Hitler's boots for four years.

That was in early July. About the same time the Denistons began talking about their coming holidays. Richie had, at the end of term, gone straight off to stay with his mother at Collioure; he would be there through August. His father and stepmother intended Scotland, where Sir Gulliver's sister's husband had a shooting lodge. Sir Gulliver's sister's name was Lady Maxwell; she possessed what Barbary remembered from infancy as an intimidating family of sons and daughters, called Molly, Joan, Kenneth, Graham, and so on, all jolly, handsome, modishly dressed, and formidably efficient at catching and killing Highland animals. Pamela too, as the time of departure approached, took on this capable Highland air. She seemed to have clothes for all emergencies and occupations that might, in the Highlands, arrive; a suit for catching salmon and trout, a suit for catching grouse, a suit for peering through telescopes at stags, a suit for playing golf, a suit, Barbary gathered, for pursuing wild goats. Since all Pamela's clothes were good, and of the kind

known as cheaper in the end, they lasted practically for
ever, leaving her coupons for stockings and shoes. She took
Barbary to her tailors, and Barbary was not surprised to
find that these were Messrs. Johnson and Brown, late of
Monkwell Street, whose old premises were now a thicket-
screened cache for black market loot. While Mr. Johnson,
or possibly it was Mr. Brown, measured her, she asked him
if he often visited his old shop.

" Unfortunately," he replied, a little stiff at the word
shop, " thanks to Herr Hitler, our former premises no
longer exist."

That's all you know, thought Barbary, relieved.

She was bored with being measured and fitted for her
tweed suit; as she only had coupons for one suit, it would
have, she supposed, to serve for the chasing of all the
creatures whom she would, no doubt, pursue.

" I don't suppose you shoot, do you? " Pamela said.

That's all you know, Barbary again silently said. I don't
suppose, she added to herself, *you've* ever sniped at Gestapo
in forests. I bet you've no Gestapo suit.

" But perhaps you fish," Pamela suggested, having heard
that the French fished all day in rivers.

" I used to go out with the nets at home," said Barbary.
"And Raoul and I fished for roach in the streams."

" Well," said Pamela, " you might get some trout in the
hill lochs. We often fish the lochs when the river isn't up
enough for salmon; it's rather good fun. . . . You'll like the
hill walks too. Molly walks a lot. Molly's eighteen, and
a very jolly girl; nice looking, too. So's Joan; she's
seventeen, and at St. Andrew's; she's going to be hockey

captain next term. The boys are at Eton; Ken's captain
of the eleven."

" Eleven what ? "

" The cricket eleven, of course." Pamela spoke a little
sharply, feeling that ignorance should have its limits. " I
say, Barbary, I advise you not to say things like that at
Arshaig. You might pretend to know just a little about
things, like other people. Even if you *have* lived abroad.
I know it's not affected, but lots of people would think it
was. . . . And you ought to get a good pair of brogues.
You can't take those frightful old canvas shoes, you know,
nor those rubber-soled sneakers you're so fond of. They'd
give the maid that does your room a fit if she saw them
about."

" I shouldn't mind her having a fit."

" Well, Cynthia would; your aunt, I mean. After all,
one does owe it to one's hostess not to come looking like
an old clothes shop or a last year's scarecrow, even if
coupons *are* short. I think you owe it to your father, too;
he's so tidy himself, and always looks smart. You know,
Barbary, you could look awfully nice, if you dressed
properly and did your hair more neatly, and didn't slouch
about the way you do. Lots of girls would like to have
your eyes and eyelashes."

" Oh, well . . ." Barbary was embarrassed, but rather
pleased.

She did not care for the distant prospect of the Highlands;
still less as it neared and acquired focus and clarity. She saw
Richie depart for Colliourc; there was no question of that
for her; perhaps never again, her waking nightmares told

83

her, against all reason, betraying her to despair. She asked her father if she might stay in London with Mrs. Cox. Sir Gulliver, vexed at such perverse nonsense, said no.

" Your aunt has particularly invited you to Arshaig. She wants you—so do I—to get to know your cousins. You've not met since you were all quite small. You'll like them very much. You'll like the place, too; there are all kinds of things to do there—fishing, boating, walking, ponies to ride, going out with the guns, sketching if you like. And I want to see something of you myself, you know; we've both been too busy for that so far."

But that, thought Barbary, would never come to much: there were too many things between them; he was clever and knew about everything, she was stupid and knew about nothing; he had taken Pamela instead of her mother, she was for ever her mother's; he stood for law and order and the police, she for the Resistance and the maquis, he for honesty and reputability, she for low life, the black market, deserters on the run, broken ruins, loot hidden in caves. All the wild, desperate squalor of the enfants du maquis years—would he even believe it if she told him? His clever, cultured, law-bound civilisation was too remote. Uneasily, she had begun to admire him; she did not want to come too near him, he would see too much; perhaps she too. She replied nothing to his last words: disappointed, he thought, She's all Helen's; she won't try to make friends with me, poor little beggar, and went off to Pamela and David. David would not be coming to Scotland; he would go with his nurse to Shanklin, to knock about with other babies and learn to paddle. Barbary thought he was lucky; he would not have to keep the high standards of Arshaig, and if he had a pair of paddling drawers they would be all the clothes he would require for hunting crab.

10

WHEN Richie arrived at the Villa Fraises, his mother was alone; Lucien Michel had just left for Toulouse after a long week-end. When could he return, he had asked, rather annoyed. Helen had replied that she didn't know yet; she must devote herself to her son for as long as he wished to stay. Will he be jealous, Lucien had asked. No, not really; not as Barbary would have been in his place; Richie is civilised, and sits lightly to people and personal relationships. But he loves me, in his easy fashion, and I him in mine, and we don't meet so often. Shall you tell him about me, Lucien had inquired. Oh, probably. I don't care for mysteries, and he had better know how I live. As you like, my dear friend. Lucien had shrugged away responsibility in the matter, and, when the day arrived, driven crossly but amicably off, his last words, Get rid of your pestilential child when you can. I never let mine interfere with my enjoyments.

But to Helen, Richie was an enjoyment in himself. She told him early about Lucien.

"Maurice's cousin; a great friend; he stays here a good deal."

Richie without difficulty grasped the rest, and changed

the subject, which was not one on which he cared to dwell, nor she.

He gave her news of Barbary.

"I'm afraid she doesn't seem to settle down much so far. Of course she misses you, and this place—anyone would. La vie civilisée has no allure for her. I gather she spends most of her time, when she's not at the Slade, painting and selling views of bomb ruins; anyhow, she isn't in the house much."

"She hasn't told me much in her letters. She writes baldly, I don't like Pamela and David, which seems a pity. Does Pamela like her, by the way?"

"Oh, well, she hardly could, much; they're too different. But she's kind enough, I think. A little annoyed at having an untaught savage for a stepdaughter, I suppose; and rather peeved that David doesn't cut more ice."

"Barbary's jealous of them both, of course. Of Pamela on my behalf, of David on Roland's. She was always jealous of Maurice; he never quite won her over, though he petted her much more than Raoul. Poor little Raoul, he was too like his mother for Maurice. . . . I believe Barbary still half thinks I might go back to your father one day, if it weren't for Pamela. She doesn't realise that my marriage was really over before I met Maurice. How do those two get on, Richie?"

"Barbary and Daddy? Both rather shy, I think. They'd like to be friends. But you and Pamela get between them, if you see what I mean."

"Did the child send me any message by you?"

"Well—not exactly." He hesitated.

" Oh, I didn't expect that she would. Did she want to come out with you ? "

" Rather badly, I think. But she said nothing. When do you want her to come, by the way ? "

" Not for some time. The life here wasn't being good for her. And she'd be jealous now of Lucien. Besides, your father wants her. No, she must learn to adjust herself to English life, my poor Barby. Perhaps by next summer . . . or perhaps I shall pay a visit to England this winter, with Roly. Yes, that might be better. To meet her away from here, and all its associations . . . I shall call and see your father. Or would he mind ? "

" I should think so."

" So do I. But we may as well be rational. I could meet Barbary somewhere else, of course, but I should rather like to see the family at home together. He's happy, isn't he ? "

" I don't really ask him. But he seems all right. He gets more and more reputation, and Pamela suits him, and runs the household well, and he likes David."

" Good. So he and I have both got the lives we prefer. We were so stupid, thinking we wanted the same kind of life."

" Yes. People keep doing that. . . . You know they're going to Arshaig in July, and taking Barbary."

Amusement twitched Helen's large mouth.

" Dear me. That will be very odd. Cynthia and those children and Barbary. I'm afraid poor Barbary will disgrace herself. I was only there once; the birds and fishes and people and guns and rods and weather and exercise bored me so much that I never went again. I used to go abroad instead; it was so much more restful. I believe, my dear, that is the point of life for me—restfulness. I suppose I am bone lazy. Like a lotos eater. Propt on beds of amaranth and moly, how sweet while warm airs lull us, et cetera. This life here suits me to the ground, because I don't have to take trouble. No one makes me go about, or dress up, or have people I don't want in my house, or work at anything. The days slide by like fruit dropping from a tree. It's so different here from that restless Riviera, with all those noisy people and that disagreeable mistral; I don't mean it never blows here, but we're sheltered. Of course, Collioure is dirty; but it's better than being smart. And this garden is paradise."

Richie agreed that it was. " But what are you writing ? " he asked, looking at the scatter of papers that littered the table by the hammock, among the glasses.

" Oh, that. It's twelfth century Provençal poetry. I'm editing it. You've heard of Geffrei, the prior of Vigeois, who's supposed to have taught Bernart of Ventodus to write troubadour poetry ? "

" Never."

" Well, he did. And there are about fifty songs by Bernart extant, but none, it was thought, by the prior. And now some manuscripts have been discovered in the crypt of the Vigeois church, signed Geffrei, and very much in Bernart's style, and I am preparing an edition of them."

" Who found them ? And where's Vigeois ? "

" I did, of course. And Vigeois is in Corrèze, not far

from Uzerche, on the Vézeré and among the Monts du
Limousin. The church is rather fine Romanesque."

"What started you looking for manuscripts in it? Tell
me about it."

"No. You can read all about it in my introduction
when it comes out. Some of the poems have been printed
already, in the *Nouvelle Revue*; they made quite a stir
among Provençal scholars."

She was smiling at him, in a way he remembered of old,
teasing, mysterious. He saw himself as a little boy, looking
up at her face in delighted doubt after some fantastic tale.
Really-truly, Mummy? Did it really-truly happen? And
the rich, deep, amused voice: Why, yes, darling, to be sure.

"Mummy," he said now, "I believe you're a fraud.
You never found any poems, did you? You've made
them up."

"Of course, dear. But don't tell anyone. It will get by
until someone wants to see the manuscripts, or wants them
returned to Vigeois. So far, no one has; which just shows
the lazy, corrupt state French Provençal scholarship has got
into. When I'm exposed I shall own up and admit it was
a hoax. I shall enjoy that. I tried the poems first on the
abbé, who was entirely taken in. People are so easily
hoaxed that I suppose it's second-rate to hoax them. But
it amuses me. I might discover a page or two of one of the
lost books of Livy next, perhaps in a battledore. Or a
treatise of Varro's, or some letters from Atticus to Cicero.
But I'm afraid classical scholars are too smart."

"Does Lucien know of your fraud?"

"Yes. I couldn't lie to Lucien. He doesn't know any-

thing about twelfth-century Provençal, but he would know
if I was deceiving him. He thinks it a good joke."

"Well, I think it's rather a bad one, actually."

"So would your father. You mustn't tell him."

"I shouldn't dream of it. But isn't it very hard work?
I mean, doesn't it mar the lazy, fruit-dropping effect of
your days?"

"No, somehow not. You know I've usually had some
private occupation on hand to entertain me, as some people
have embroidery, or patience. It passes the time agreeably."

"I think you're so odd, mama. Because you really are
a scholar; and yet you've none of the scholar's conscience."

"I've no conscience of any kind, my dear. It seems to
have been left out of me. It's a pity; I should be a nicer
person if I had one. But as to scholars, you'll agree that
many of them have had extremely odd and capricious
consciences, even about their particular subject. Fraud,
forgery, plagiarism, falsification, theft, concealment and
even destruction of documents, to win glory or to prove a
theory—scholars of all periods have done that kind of thing.
Look at Leonardo Aretino and what he did; and that doctor
to a convent who stole Cicero's treatise on glory, used it in
his own book, and then destroyed it. It was common form
during the Renaissance, when they kept fishing up from
cellars manuscripts lost for centuries, or finding them in
markets wrapped round fish. And look at Gregory VIII,
keeping up Augustine's credit by burning the works he had
plagiarised from. As for Aristotle, he was so ill-treated and
mauled about by his Greek and Roman copyists that we
can scarcely be sure of anything he wrote. And I could

91

tell you some of the deeds of scholars during the last fifty years that would shock you. Plenty of them are alive to-day —I could give you their names—burrowing away like moles in libraries and holding forth in common rooms looking as if butter wouldn't melt in their mouths. I hope I look like that myself."

" No. I think you look as if it would."

" A pity. Though I don't really see why the innocent should have refrigerator mouths and the guilty hot ones."

" How old are you, mummy? I forget."

" What a question, dear! Forty-four. Why? "

" I was only thinking, it's a little odd that you should be a crook. Someone was saying the other day that it's the people under forty who've taken to swindling and lying in a big way, and that the middle-aged people, if they were well brought up, remain more or less incorrupt. My friends are nearly all crooks; they cheat the customs and lie and black market and buy petrol and clothes coupons; but their parents say they can't throw off their early training, which taught them that, whatever else gentlemen and ladies might do, they mustn't cheat. *I* cheat freely; I smuggled home three watches and six pairs of socks and two bottles of brandy last time I came to France; and this time I sold my gold studs in Paris, and mean to soak you for many thousands of francs. Do *you* cheat the customs? "

" I don't know; I haven't crossed any frontiers lately. I dare say I should, though. One had so much practice in lying during the occupation. It became the right thing to do. Children like Barbary and Raoul will never recover from it; but then they ran round with the maquis. After all, when you're up against torturers and tyrants, you have to adapt yourself. Yes, I expect I should cheat the customs, or the government, as well as Provençal scholars. Not at cards, though; I should draw the line at that, it's so easily seen through. Your father, naturally, would never cheat at all. Nor, I imagine, would his new wife, though she is a long way under forty?"

"No, I don't think she would. She's terribly upright and Roedean."

"I suppose that's where we ought to have sent Barbary, instead of the Slade. But I expect they'd have expelled her after the first week. Oh, well, she'll probably marry a crook, so it would be no good her setting herself up to be honest. It's a world of crooks now, and however many of them people like your father send to gaol, there'll be more outside. The crook in all of us is bursting out and taking possession, like Hyde, while Jekyll slowly dies of attrition. I dare say you and your spiv friends will be cat-burgling soon."

"I expect we shall. Murdering too, would you say, or is that another line of development? I don't really feel violent, even after my four years training in dreadful deeds."

"Oh, murder comes too. Not to you, I think; you're much more likely to react from violence into gentleness and an elegant dolce far niente civilisation. But to those who don't react from violence, murder comes too."

Her voice had dropped a tone. Looking at her, he saw that she had become suddenly grave; the spinning of the human race down the ringing grooves of crime had left the realm of entertaining speculation, and had taken a grim, bitter, authentic note.

"Well," he said, "I shall stay a gentle, civilised, swindling crook. I hope I shall do well at it and make my fortune."

"We shall none of us do well," she returned, still grave. "We shall all go down and down into catastrophe and the abyss. We must snatch what good we can on the way. So I idle here in the sun and enjoy my chosen life and amusements while I can, and send away one child for her good, and keep another with me for my pleasure, and enjoy the third when he comes my way, and refuse to waste my time on people or occupations that bore me, and get along, on the whole, pretty well, even though the best is over for me."

Daddy? he asked himself for a moment; then answered, No, Maurice. No one will ever take his place with her. The others will only fill a gap and pass the time. Poor mother,

"Another drink, darling?" She filled two glasses, and lifted one. "Here's to our successful crookery. May we both make our fortunes. And here's to Barbary at Arshaig among the salmon."

11

ARSHAIG, in the western Highlands, was very beautiful. Purple skies came down to meet a purple waste of heather; a shining river in which salmon bounced and hid among rocks in deep pools wound through the moors; brown burns tumbled singing from the hills; steel-pale lochs, holding the light, and whispering with tall reeds, lay hidden in folds and dips of purple mountains; rough tracks climbed like winding brown ribbons through the heather, from hamlet to hill farm, from crofter's cottage to mountain loch. Highland cattle roamed shaggily through the heather.

The Maxwells' shooting lodge stood in a fold of the moors, half a mile from an elbow of the river, with oak and beech woods at its back and a well-planned garden in front, where bright flowers bloomed in beds beneath smooth gravel paths and fruit trees climbed walls and a fountain played in a water-lily pond. The lodge was low and long and grey; its two wings sheltered the garden, and behind it were the outhouses, garages and yard, where a good many dogs of the chase strolled about or sat in kennels barking; Sir Angus Maxwell and his children knew all their names, as also those of the ponies, the gillies, the keepers, the river pools, the hills, the lochs, and the shepherds and crofters for miles round. Lady Maxwell knew also those of all the roses and other plants in the garden and greenhouses. The whole family loved Arshaig very dearly, and spent as much time there as Sir Angus could spare from his professional duties, which were those of a consulting specialist in nerve ailments. He had become so eminent in this line that he was frequently called in by worried statesmen and monarchs, superseded generals, defeated parliamentary candidates, jealous wives, over-worked hostesses and business men, under-worked actors and actresses for whom resting proved too distressing, and authors suffering from libel actions or neglect. Sir Angus's view was that everyone suffered from nervous ailments, it was part of the normal human lack of equipment for life, but that some were easily curable, some negligible, and some destructive, if neglected, of reason. He had decided that the Scots were peculiarly addicted to such ailments, and set this down partly to race, partly to climate, and partly to the rugged expanse of mountain landscape and heather with which many of them were surrounded, and which, though beautiful, was awful, and started fantasies and fears. Women and girls, whether in Scotland or elsewhere, he regarded as seldom completely curable; their normal condition was that of nervous instability, and all he could do for them was to steady them to a point where, among other women and girls, they would pass muster. Secretly, though admitting degrees, he believed them practically all a little mad; you never knew when their nerves would not suddenly break, and precipitate them into some kind of abyss. His wife, Sir Gulliver's sister, outwardly calm, was liable, like her distinguished brother, to tense fits of brittle self-control and ill-suppressed annoyance. His two girls could only with difficulty sustain without nervous deterioration, the excitements, disappointments, triumphs and fatigues of their lives; the boys, on the other hand, went through these with the tough tranquillity that distinguishes a large part of English male youth.

And now here was Gulliver's girl Barbary, that mournful-eyed waif from an unhappy France and a dissolute mother, looking as if she might at any moment crack.

"Cheerful society," his brother-in-law told him, "and healthy exercise, are what the child needs. To run about the moors for a few weeks with your children will do her a lot of good. She can fish the lochs and ride the pony and shoot an odd rabbit if she cares to. She's been too much absorbed in her painting lately. And she misses her mother and that French place. She's shy of us here; I haven't got the key to her. Perhaps she's been turned against us . . . not deliberately, I don't suppose; Helen wouldn't bother or care, and, to do her justice, she was never malicious; but a child absorbs an atmosphere. Of course too, they must have had a disturbing time during the occupation— Germans, the Vichy police, the Resistance, the need to steer a course between suspected collaboration and arrest. No doubt they saw a lot of their acquaintances being taken away. She never tells me a word about all that; but I imagine she had a lot to scare her, one way and another. Her mother's tough, nothing ever scared her; but Barbary's different. And here she is, on my hands, my responsibility, and I haven't really a clue. I suppose I don't easily make friends with young people; anyhow, I have no time in London. I'd like to make something of it here, if she'll let me."

Looking that evening at his wife's niece, as she sat at dinner between Joan and Kenneth, Sir Angus thought of a wild strayed kitten which has stepped into a strange house and glances about it with wary slate-grey eyes. Yes, he thought, she's been scared all right. Pretty badly, I should guess, and it's left its mark. There's something more there, too. . . . Unless something happens to reverse the gear, she may be heading for a breakdown. And there she is, stuck in London with those two. He looked at his brother-in-law, fastidious, delicate-featured and faintly aloof, amusing the company with some court-room story, and at Pamela, handsome, cheerful and unperceptive, five months gone with her second child.

She needs her mother, Sir Angus thought, remembering the pair as he had seen them together long ago. Confound the woman, chucking her job like that. Recollecting how singularly ill, on the whole, she had performed that job, he could scarcely wish her back at it; but she ought not to have taken Barbary with her into that dubious, disintegrating life. He determined to talk to her, win her confidence, discover what ailed her, show Gulliver, whom he suspected of thinking psychologists foolish, vain, and second-rate, what penetration into the human mind was theirs.

12

RIDING Jock the pony up the moor track to Loch Dubh with Molly and Hugh, Barbary thought, this would make a good maquis, for the purple heather swelled and rolled about them knee high, and the bog myrtle made patches of blue-green, and clumps of birches and rocks stood together, and rabbits jumped across the sandy track. Hugh shot at them; there would be plenty to eat, thought Barbary when they sat by their camp-fires in the evenings.

The track bent round a shoulder of hill, and there before them lay Loch Dubh, small, silver and reedy, with a boat shack at the near end. A light breeze ribbed the glassy surface; curlews cried round it. The track dipped down to the rushy edge; they tied up the pony, got out the boat, and pushed it into rippling grey water. They thought it would be a good afternoon for fishing, not too bright, not too smooth. All three had rods; they rowed out into the middle and drifted. Barbary fished from the bows; trout jumped and plumped about, devouring live flies, snapping at, rejecting and occasionally swallowing bogus ones, dragging the lines down among reeds and mud. A few were landed before the morning breeze dropped and the loch lay transparent and smooth. Then they rowed in and

ate their sandwiches, and sat down to wait for the afternoon
ripple. Barbary, who had caught nothing and was clumsy
with a trout rod, said she was tired of fishing, she would
ride about the moors instead. They told her to hold Jock's
head up so that he would not stumble into rabbit holes.

"I expect she won't, all the same," Hugh said, watching
her go. "I think she's awfully careless."

Barbary rode off into the grey and purple lands that
swelled about her beneath the misty sky. This was truly a
maquis, stretching from hill to hill, from slope to hollow,
a tangled waste of pink ling, red bell heather, green bog,
jutting rocks, and clumps of birch and pine forest for
cover. Jock ambled along the narrow paths between the
heather, his rider astride on his back, his reins hanging
loosely from her hands, her bare legs dangling against his
rough flanks. He perceived that he had *carte blanche* to take
her wherever he liked, so made for Kiltulloch farm on the
slopes of Ben Dubh, where his mother lived and where
he had been born. Kiltulloch was three miles away; sometimes a bend in the path would show it, a low grey
farmhouse standing high among firs.

Both happy, they ambled on. Barbary whistled a
Roussillon fisherman's song, snapping the fingers of one
hand over her head; Molly and Hugh, catching sight of
her from the loch, were confirmed in their view that she
was more than a little mad. They hoped she would bring
Jock safely back.

The sun came out of the mist, flies hummed in the
heather, midges and gnats and horse flies crowded round
and bit; Barbary waved bracken about her like a fan.

They came to a burn; Jock waded across it, Barbary slid
off him and paddled among little trout, an action for which
the Kiltulloch farm children would have been skelped.
As she sat on a rock dangling her legs in a pool, triumphant
clucking sounded from somewhere; it was apparent that
a hen had laid a shell egg. When hens clucked Barbary
and Raoul and their companions had always been used to
pursue the sound and take the eggs before anyone else did
so. Automatically Barbary looked about her; the clucking
seemed to come from a fir copse beyond the burn. She
pulled on her alpargatars, which she had brought to Scotland
and wore when Pamela was not there to stop her, and went
off through the heather, leaving Jock to his devices. The
clucking led her to the fir copse, which was circumvallated
by a stout wire fence. Surmounting this hindrance, Barbary
pushed through bracken and heather, starting large and
grandiose birds from their afternoon rest; they chattered
and squawked as they flew up. The hen sat in the middle
of a clump of fern, rolling on Barbary a malevolent beady
eye; when Barbary groped beneath her she pecked her
arm. Barbary drew from the nest two large brown shell
eggs, dropped one into each pocket of her shorts, and
crawled away, the bracken waving and closing over her
like green water disturbed.

"Hey!" Raucous cries broke the afternoon peace;
heavy footsteps crashed about the heather; two voices
exclaimed to one another in Gaelic, no more to be understood than the German of the soldiers in France; it had a
similar alien ferocity. It conveyed to Barbary that she had
been perceived and was being hunted down. Pulling out

a catapult from its pocket in her belt, she fitted it with a small fir cone and, still crouched in bracken, took a sight on a small fierce Highland farmer who was scrambling over the wire fence, and let fly at a bright red face. It struck him beneath the eye; with a cry of rage and pain he clapped his hand to the spot, while his companion, a younger man with less of the Gael in his aspect and speech, jumped down into the copse, strode to the predatory menace crouched in the fern, and yanked her to her feet.

"Hey! It's a lassie!" he cried, while the slight, disreputable, flannel-shorted figure writhed and twisted to get free of the firm grip on its shoulder. He dragged it to the wire fence and over it, plumping it on the heather before his angry father, who was still chafing his bruised eye.

"A lassie!" he echoed. "So it's you are the thief robbing my hens and shooting my eye. Donal, she has an egg to each pocket."

Donal extracted these, both by now cracked and leaking, and took possession of the catapult.

"And where do you come from, you young rascal, and who may you be?"

Barbary said nothing: one did not give information of that kind when caught; not a word, whatever they did to one; that was the first principle of the maquis. Not that most people were able to obey it to the end; it was known that the breaking point came sooner or later; that was why plans and meeting places were changed so often. But silence under questioning became a habit. She stood sullenly between them, staring down at the heather.

"I take it the lassie's a visitor," Donal pronounced. "She's no from hereabouts."

"Speak out, will you, you limber," his injured father adjured, "or ye'll feel this stick across your legs."

Barbary kept her mouth tightly shut.

Donal, looking round, exclaimed, "Hey, Da! There's Jock ganging up to the house, looking for his mither. The lassie must have ridden him over from Arshaig. Did ye no?"

Barbary shook her head.

"You're a bonny liar, lass," the farmer told her. "It's at Arshaig you are, though ye dinna look it. By the looks of ye, ye could come off one o' them sharrybang tours that drive fra' Glasgow carrying a rabble from over the border, the half o' them got up in kilts and the other half in shorties, and not ane o' them ken how to act in heather or in burns, tramping aboot distairbing the birds in the woods and wading in the trout pools. But gin you're stopping at Arshaig, I'll be there mysel the morn to speak to Sir Angus aboot ye. Ye'll no be ane o' his lassies, for I've kenned them baith since they were wee bairns, and I've no fault to find with either. It's not they would go stealing eggs and shooting a man in the eye with fir cones on his ain land. Aye, we'll see what Sir Angus has to say the morn."

"I don't know Sir Angus. That's not where I'm staying. I came off a charabanc from Glasgow"

"Then what are ye doing with our Jock saddled and running after ye? Maybe ye've stolen him too. Ye're a liar and a thief, lassie, and forbye ye tried to kill me too.

If the constable lived near by I'd hand ye over to him, but he's awa' beyond Craig Dubh. Now you be riding back on Jock, and ye can tell Sir Angus I'll be calling on him."

Barbary rode down again to Loch Dubh. She was not much disconcerted; such incidents, among her and Raoul and their friends, were common, and often complained of by the farmers of the Sorède.

Molly and Hugh were out in the boat; the breeze was stirring again and the fish rising; innocent and well behaved, they flogged the rippling loch. They would never poach in other people's waters, other people's woods. They called to Barbary, did she want to come out? She said no, and waded among the reeds by the edge with a landing net, looking for minnows in the mud.

* 13 *

"**B**UT why," Sir Angus asked, " did you *want* the eggs
exactly ? "

Mr. Macdougall from Kiltulloch had been and gone, in
a heat of reasonable indignation; he had made his complaint, shown his bruised eye, handed Sir Angus the
catapult, received apologies, and ridden away. Sir Angus
had summoned Barbary, who now sat opposite him in
the library, opposing to interrogation a blank, expressionless
face.

" I suppose," she answered, " to eat. We always went
to get the eggs when we heard a hen. Don't you ? "

" By no means, unless it happens to be my hen. Still,
let that pass. Why did you proceed to catapult Mr.
Macdougall in the eye ? It was really very dangerous;
you might have injured him seriously."

" I suppose," Barbary explained, " it was just that he was
coming, and might have caught me."

" As, in point of fact, he did. A rather drastic method
of self-defence, surely. Was that the way you treated your
neighbours in France ? "

" Well, not most of them. The Germans. And the
Vichy police. And the collabos."

" I see. Mr. Macdougall, of course, is neither German,

105

Vichy, nor collabo. What you mean is, I suppose, that such a reaction to approaching enemies has become a habit. And naturally the owner of land on which one is trespassing and of property which one is purloining must be regarded as an enemy. But you know where such aggression might land you? In a police court."

A flicker passed over Barbary's impassivity. Fear, he noted, observing her. She was frightened of the police. She possessed no one of the four freedoms. Least of all, freedom of speech.

" Well," he said, " never mind it now. Mr. Macdougall has been kind enough to overlook it. I think he supposed you not more than fourteen, and I didn't enlighten him. So we can let it go at that, though I hope, for the sake of my good relations with my neighbours, that it won't occur again. . . . By the way, there are a lot of things I should be interested to hear about your life in France under the occupation. It must have been pretty grim in many ways."

Barbary said nothing; she looked at him with startled, uneasy eyes.

" I thought," said Sir Angus, " that you might possibly like to talk about it, sometime or other. It must be on your mind a good deal, I imagine. Inevitably, of course. Yes, we must talk of it. I think you would feel better afterwards. That, you know, is the way we get rid of things that are worrying us. . . . How about coming out fishing with me to-morrow? I am walking up to Loch Glentire. I won't take anyone else, if you would care to come."

He looked at her with penetrating eyes, as if, while they walked over the heather, he would discern everything that had happened to her in her life. With all the practice he had, he probably would do so.

"Thank you, Uncle Angus." She admired him; she felt what the patients in his consulting room no doubt felt, that to talk to him would bring a fatal ease, an end to concealment, a drowsy numbness as though of hemlock she had drunk. So she had felt before, years before (how many years? Two?) when keen eyes had searched her, questioning, demanding answers, trying persuasion before threats, before pain. . . . But before pain she had told nothing; it was during pain, after pain, that she had spoken, and told —what? Darkness rolled in on memory and mind, a confused, saving oblivion, swinging shut a door.

Sir Angus said: " Good. We'll start at eleven."

He went away to fish for salmon in the river, feeling pleased that to-morrow he would probe the dark places in the obviously disarranged mind of his wife's niece. A helpful doctor, he would like to cure the poor child, and also to show his brother-in-law that psychologists knew their job and could cure people in ways of which the law was ignorant.

* 14 *

GREY dawn misted the Arshaig hills; the lochs lay about
them like steel and silver medallions; a small chill
wind whispered among the heather. Darkness and secrecy,
the misty, dreaming twilight of the western Highlands.

Arshaig Lodge, as yet sleeping and shut, lay shadowed
on the hill slope; before it its flower garden raised bright
banners on green strips of sward; beads of mist jewelled
orange, blue and scarlet petals, which gleamed like coral,
sapphire and amber in a jungle of wet green seaweed.
Behind the winged grey lodge, beyond the sleeping stables,
outhouses, kennels and yard, the fruit garden rambled, the
peas and beans, the unripe fruit against the wall, the late
Scotch strawberries red beneath their nets. Along the
paved path between the strawberries and currants came
Barbary, treading silently in rope-soled shoes, stopping
once to pick ripe strawberries where they gleamed through
the net. She wore brown corduroy slacks and a leather
jacket, and carried a rucksack on her back; her coat
pockets bulged. She looked wan and heavy eyed, as if she
had not slept; furtively she glanced about her as she
climbed the stile that shut the garden from the hillside.
She crossed the wooden bridge over the burn and took to

the heather; it pushed wet about her legs as she trod the
narrow track that twisted down the hill. The shaggy
forelocked heads and great wild horns of Highland cattle
tossed about in the mist; the gentlest, she had been told,
of the cattle kind. She followed the burn down; the little
sound of its going gurgled through the dark dawn; curlews
rose up and cried like the wind in the straining sails of
ships, or like lost owls. Here was a maquis, for anyone
who had a mind to take to it, for anyone escaping, plotting
or hiding. Was there a secret multitude lurking in it? Did
they lurk and shelter in the ruined hamlets of departed
crofters, those roofless, empty grey walls tumbling into
oblivion on the hills, where sheep cropped the sparse turf?
Probably they did so; perhaps secret eyes even now peered
from the heather, watching the alien wayfarer, while quiet
whispers hushed and shushed from one to another as she
passed. Going through a clump of birch, Barbary saw a
blackened patch and a tripod of sticks, where a pot or
kettle had not long since simmered over a fire; it recalled
to her the camping places they had used in the Forêt de
Sorède. In this maquis, too, were the lurkers on the margin,
who hid from cities and made fires in the heather.

But they were unknown, they were strange, she had
no contacts with them. She must go, she knew, to another
margin, another maquis, to the flowering wilderness and
broken ruins that she knew. She must go far from Arshaig,
from its disconcerting alien standards and from the searching
eyes that looked into her mind, trying to read it, questioning
and surmising, dragging her thoughts as with a deep-sea
net. An hour of such dragging, and all the fish would be

hauled in, would flow in of themselves, almost relieved to be caught. Things would be told, would be guessed, that must never be told, never be guessed. Things would be dragged up that must lie for ever in the deep, secret pools of the sea, till some tide at last washed them out into the ocean of oblivion, never to be captured more.

Until that should happen, Barbary was going back where she belonged, to the waste margins of civilisation that she knew, where other outcasts lurked, and questions were not asked.

* 15 *

SIR ANGUS waited in the garden, carefully assembling his flies, for he was of those who believe that trout discriminate greatly between one artificial fly and another. The rest of the party were gone out to kill animals, except Pamela, who, on account of her condition, sometimes took days off from this pastime and stayed in the house and garden. She was at this moment employing herself usefully in the flower-beds, with gardening gloves and clippers. Sir Angus, glancing at her with approval, thought what a fine handsome young woman she was, and how useful in the garden, and how very much better Gulliver had done with his second wife than his first.

" Have you seen Barbary? " he presently asked her. " She's coming out with me."

Pamela replied that she had not seen Barbary all the morning; she must have gone out early, for she had not shown up at breakfast.

" Well," Sir Angus said, " we arranged to start at eleven."

" Oh, Barbary's never on time. She scarcely knows what the word means. She never bothers about other people's convenience, I'm afraid. She'll turn up at any time that happens to suit her. I shouldn't wait, if I were you."

" I shall wait half an hour." Sir Angus consulted his watch. " After that, if she hasn't turned up, I shall conclude that she doesn't mean to, and go without her. I shan't be surprised. I guessed that she might shy at a walk alone with me when she thought it over." He continued to sort flies, whistling under his breath, considering whether it was worth while to try and get a little light on his subject from this competent and rather obtuse young woman. Having decided that it was, and that the illumination would doubtless shed even more light on the young woman herself (light on all human beings was what it was his hobby to seek), he said, in casually idle tone, " Is she happy here, should you say ? "

" I've no idea." The shears briskly snipped off dead flowers. " I've no clue to what Barbary feels about anything. She doesn't talk to *me*, you know. Nor to Gully."

That, at least, gives you satisfaction, Sir Angus thought.

" If she does to you," Pamela went on, " you'll be highly favoured, I assure you."

" Then you've neither of you so far succeeded in winning her confidence ? "

" Oh, I don't suppose I've tried particularly. She's Gully's child, not mine. I'm sure she doesn't want me tagging after her. I fancy she's pretty jealous of me, being in her mother's place and all that. It's natural, if you come to think of it. I expect we both feel the less we see of each other the better, so long as we get on decently together, of course, and I take care we do that. But she's not the sort of girl I should ever have made friends with particularly, even if the position wasn't what it is."

" No ? "

" No. She isn't open or straightforward, and I can't do with that. And she really is most peculiar in lots of ways. Rambling about London by herself, or with that Michel boy she sometimes brings to the house, which I must say seems rather poor taste, considering everything. I can't think what they do or where they go. He looks as sly and secretive as she does. Then, the way she dresses. Dirty old canvas shoes, as often as not, and tears in her frocks that she never mends. She comes in often looking as if she'd been dragged through a bramble bush. Gully doesn't like it, as you can imagine; he keeps asking me to see to her clothes, but I can't go with her everywhere and keep her from getting into a mess. Her mother must have let her run wild and do exactly what she liked. Was *she* untidy too ? "

" Helen ? No. Untidy couldn't be the word for her, ever. Nor, I admit, could tidy. She wore her clothes as if she didn't know or care what she had on—and looked magnificent always. Something like a goddess in a leopard skin. Or possibly Cleopatra. Carelessly, lazily superb."

" I see." A little annoyed, Pamela snipped off a flower not yet withered. " Well, whatever she looked like, she hasn't taught Barbary manners. Nor behaviour. You know, it's an awful pity she isn't a year or two younger; then she could have gone away to school and learned to behave like other people instead of like a guttersnipe."

Sir Angus realised that his description of Helen was largely responsible for the sharpness of the last word, and for the execution of the rose in bloom.

"Still," he said, "I suppose Gully wants her at home for a time, to get to know her."

"She worries him a lot. With all his work on his mind, he oughtn't to be worried. It would be better for him if she could be away somewhere. For one thing, her being there reminds him of things—of all that awful time he had before. I want him to forget all that, and be cheerful with David and me. And it's all right for him to be with Richie, too. Richie's very sweet always, and fits in."

"Richie's with his mother for the summer, isn't he?"

"Yes. I think he felt he ought to go out to her. In a way it's a pity, because he might have done something with Barbary. She's better with him than with us—less sulky."

"She wasn't sulky as a child. I remember her a high-spirited little girl, delighted with riding the pony, and with her first pocket-knife. Gully says she misses her mother a good deal. That may partly account for what you call sulkiness."

"Of course she misses her. She's crazy about her. That's why she hates me, I suppose. Apparently she thinks her father ought to have sat down and waited meekly for years in case her mother should ever see fit to leave her other men and come back to him. She won't so much as look at David; she looks at him as if she didn't think he should have been born. It makes me wild, I must say. Richie says she dotes on her French baby stepbrother. I daren't leave David alone with her, she might pinch him or something."

"You think badly of her, I observe."

"Well, don't you? After that escapade yesterday with the catapult——"

"Maquis manners, that's all. I think she's nervy, and not very happy, and has a good deal on her mind which she would like to forget and can't. I would like to help her, if I can. But one's got to understand her state of mind first, not just dismiss it as sulks."

"You know she steals?" Pamela sharply returned.

"Likely enough. More maquis manners."

"Oh, well, put it down to that if you like. *I* should say she takes after her mother. After all, she—Helen, I mean—did gamble away thousands of pounds of Gully's money. I don't know if Barbary gambles, she probably hasn't the wits. But she certainly takes money and food from the house. What she does with it I don't know. I rather guess she and that boy mix with some pretty doubtful company. I suppose really I ought to try and find out, but I can't go snooping. Besides, I don't feel up to much at present. So I let her go her own way, and try to keep Gully from getting worried. I only hope she won't get into some real scrape and land in a police court. I mean, if she steals from us, she may steal from other people, for all one knows—shops, or people's handbags. . . . It's not very nice, you know, Angus, thinking when she's out of all the awful things she may be doing."

"I shouldn't worry. It's not your business to."

"It's Gully I'm thinking of. He'd feel so awful. I mean, being a K.C. and all that would make it worse. He'd never get over it if she did get into disgrace. . . . I can't help wishing she'd stayed in France with her mother. She'd have been happier, and so should we. But Gully felt he ought to have her with him for a time."

"He used to be devoted to her when she was a little girl."

"I dare say. He's fond of children. He *adores* David. And, if he wants a little girl to pet, perhaps this next one will be that; I think he hopes so. Whichever it is, it will give him much less trouble than Barbary does."

"Very probably. . . . Well, I don't think I shall wait any more. If Barbary turns up later, tell her I was sorry to miss her. We must have our walk another day."

Through the afternoon and evening the family drifted home, laden heavily or lightly with trophies of the chase. Sir Gulliver had a large salmon, which he had played for two hours in the Long Pool; Kenneth had hooked a sea-trout in the burn, which had finally broken his line and got away; Molly and Joan had a creel full of small trout from Loch Dubh; Hugh had two rabbits; Lady Maxwell a basket full of cuttings from the garden of the friends with whom she had lunched. Sir Angus had found the waters of Loch Glentire too clear; the fish he had angled for had seen their peril and eluded it, taking evasive action among reeds and mud, which he took to be symbolic.

* 16 *

Over a large late tea they all recounted to one another their triumphs and their disappointments, the creatures they had captured and the creatures who had escaped them. Sir Angus came in last, with his empty creel.

" Is Barbary back yet ? " he asked.

It seemed that no one had seen Barbary.

" She rather enjoys long days out by herself," her father said. " She turns up all right in the end. I don't suppose she even took a rod; she likes just rambling about."

" I do hope," said Lady Maxwell, " that she hasn't lost herself. It's quite easy, on the moors. You shouldn't have let her go off alone, children."

The children explained that their cousin was already gone out when they came down to breakfast.

" Oh, she'll be all right," Sir Gulliver said, a little uneasily, because Barbary might be stealing shell eggs somewhere, or catapulting farmers, shepherds, or sheep, or actually lost, or lying with a sprained ankle on the hills.

" I might go out and look for her," he added. " But, as no one knows which way she went, it would probably be waste of time."

117

Sir Angus went to his study to write letters. His wife presently came to him there.

" Angus, such a tiresome thing. My notecase is missing, with fifteen pounds in it. I've only just discovered it. So stupid of me, I left it last night in a drawer in my writing bureau and forgot to lock it. I'm afraid Maggie. . . . Of course she's very young, and hasn't been with us long, and I suppose the temptation was too much for her. But what shall I say to make her admit it? How I dislike these things ! "

" Say nothing yet," Sir Angus told her. " You don't know it was Maggie, and we can't assume it."

" Well, it couldn't be Mrs. Fraser or Chrissie. And I can't believe any of the men came upstairs. Maggie really seems the only possibility. And it's no use leaving it too long. Shall I consult Gully, do you think ? "

Lady Maxwell, when it came to crime, put her trust more in K.C.s than in psychological doctors, whom she did not believe to know so much about the less admirable side of human nature, or to deal with it so effectively.

But Sir Angus said no, she had better not consult Gully, nor, at present, anyone else.

" Leave it alone for a time," he advised. " Talking about it may do harm."

Lady Maxwell said she couldn't see what harm, and while they were not talking the fifteen pounds might be spent.

Sir Angus said it was very probably largely spent already. Lady Maxwell asked if he thought Maggie had already gone shopping in the village or had perhaps passed the

money over to some young man. Sir Angus said he had
not mentioned Maggie, and hoped that she would not do
so either. It would, he said, be most unjust, without
evidence of Maggie's guilt.

"My dear, she's the only possible suspect. It isn't as if
we still had Miss What's-her-name."

Miss What's-her-name, an intoxicated secretary they had
once had, with the most candid blue eyes, had broken open
locked drawers and finally departed without leaving her
address, having cashed on her employers a post-dated
cheque for ten pounds which proved to be a dud. But this
had been long before "everyone had grown so dishonest,"
as Lady Maxwell complained; perhaps, she sometimes
thought, such secretarial activities were common form in
these days, now that the war had so reduced moral standards.
How on earth, she wondered, in common with many
others, will people be behaving after yet another war,
should one occur?

Dinner-time arrived, in the full daylight that makes
evenings in the Highlands so delightful and odd. The
Maxwells did not pander to summer time, single or double,
except when catching steamers or trains, so that dinner was
not till the hour which most people called half-past nine.
At half-past eight Sir Gulliver, who was hitting a captive
golf ball in the garden, was joined by his brother-in-law.

"I think I had better tell you," said Sir Angus, "that
Barbary has probably gone off somewhere by boat or
train."

"You think so? Why? I don't think she had much

money on her—so far as I know. Not enough, I mean, to get far."

" I think she may have had. There's some missing from Cynthia's bureau, which it's possible she may have taken for the journey."

" Cynthia's bureau? She wouldn't do that."

" Are you sure? I'm not accusing her; but, in the nervy and disordered state she seems to be in, mightn't she help herself to money she found about, if she needed it? Has she ever done it before? Pamela told me she had."

" Pamela told you. . . ." His fine-cut mouth tightened. After a moment he said, quietly: " I'm sorry Pamela talks like that about Barbary. I shouldn't have supposed that she would. . . . Of course things haven't been particularly easy between them; naturally. The position is difficult. Natural incompatibility, and perhaps some jealousy on both sides. And Pam's state of health just now. . . . She has told me sometimes that Barbary takes things from the house— money and food. But after all, it's the child's home. It's very different from taking money from here. . . .Was it lying about? "

" Not exactly. It was in a drawer. I don't think you need take it too seriously, if she did do it. The past few years have had a queer effect on a great many people, young and older. And she has had, I gather, a rather ungoverned bringing up in France, running about with young resisters to whom anything was right that might injure the authorities. That habit of mind isn't easily lost. The only importance of this, if she has done it, is that it looks as if she had planned a journey. Would she go to London, do you think? "

" I suppose she might. Mrs. Cox is in the house. I don't know why she should want to, though."

" Many possible reasons suggest themselves. She may have felt shy here, a fish out of water, among relations she scarcely knows. She may have been ashamed of herself, after Macdougall's complaint. And she may have wanted to avoid me. You see, I had asked her to come out with me to-day in order to get her to talk to me about herself and her doings."

" What for? " Sir Gulliver regarded his brother-in-law as too inquisitive.

" Because I saw that, if she didn't talk to someone, make a clean breast of whatever was bothering her, anything might happen."

" Well, as you know, I haven't your faith in talk as a cure. People sometimes talk themselves deeper into a mess, when they'd have got out of it all right if they'd kept their mouths shut. In my profession, we always warn our clients not to run round talking about their affairs. If Barbary didn't want to chatter about hers, she showed some sense. Still, she needn't have run away. I suppose I must ring up Mrs. Cox to-morrow and find out if she's there. It's no use my going there till I know; she may be anywhere. She may be back here to-night, or to-morrow. In fact, I quite expect it. Then she'll be able to clear up this business about the money. Meanwhile, I shall go out now and search the moors. I shall walk up to Loch Dubh first. Don't keep any dinner for me; I'll take sandwiches with me. I may be out till late."

"Before you start," said Sir Angus, "I shall telephone to Ardrishaig and ask if anyone happened to see her take the Glasgow boat."

Sir Gulliver went upstairs. In their bedroom Pamela was changing for dinner.

"What exactly," he asked her, "have you been saying to Angus about Barbary?"

She answered casually, "Nothing in particular. He talked to me about her; asked questions, wanted to know about her. I don't know why. I helped him as far as I could."

"By telling him she stole?"

"Yes, among other things. Oh, it's quite safe with Angus, he won't let it go any further. He thinks he can help her, and after all, he's a kind of doctor. So I thought he'd better know more about her."

"I see. Well, you've apparently convinced him that she's a thief. Now he thinks she has taken some money from a drawer and made off with it."

"Is there some missing? Well, I expect she has."

"Why should you expect it, without a shred of evidence? Please oblige me, Pamela, by not talking like that, either to me or to anyone else."

Stung by the sharpness of his tone, she hit back.

"Barbary is entirely dishonest, and you know she is. It's no use being an ostrich about it. She's been badly brought up, and isn't to be trusted. What else she does I've no idea; but I do know she steals from the house.

Money, food (apart from what Mrs. Cox hands out to her) and I'm pretty sure my ration book and clothes coupons that disappeared, though I couldn't prove it. I lock everything I can now."

Meeting Gulliver's eyes in the glass, she saw his face contract and tighten with anger.

"That's enough, Pamela." He left the room, quietly shutting the door behind him.

I've made him cross, thought his wife. But he'd better know what she is, I'm not going to pretend. Perhaps when he really sees through her he'll send her back to France. Then we shall all be happier. If she goes on worrying us as she's been doing for the last four months, baby may be born a monster.

Sir Angus was telephoning in the hall. He hung up the receiver as his brother-in-law came downstairs.

" She was seen on the pier by the ticket office people, or someone very like her, going on to the Gourock boat with a rucksack. I think we may take it that she got to Glasgow, and probably caught the night train to Euston. So it's scarcely worth while looking for her round here; do you agree? "

Sir Gulliver stood uncertainly; he looked tired.

" I suppose so. You think it's pretty certain, then? "

" I should say quite. A girl alone, in corduroy trousers and canvas shoes, rather small, pale, with dark hair on her shoulders and a rucksack. It seems there weren't many passengers getting on at Ardrishaig, and someone in the ticket office happened to notice her. As you know, it's what I expected myself."

123

" All right. Then for the moment there seems nothing to be done. I shall telephone to the house in the morning, and catch the midday boat."

17

A<small>T</small> nine o'clock next evening Barbary rang the bell in Adelphi Terrace. Mrs. Cox let her in, with ejaculations of satisfaction.

"Whatever have you been doing, love? Your Pa's been phoning me from Scotland about you; he began at nine this morning, wanting to know if you'd come on the night train, which he had reason, he said, to believe you had. I was to let him know the minute you turned up. Poor gentleman, he was right down worried. What have you been up to now, you little monkey? Now you tell Coxy all about it, while I get you some supper. I've just had mine, I had my daughter and her husband in and a few friends, just for a bit of company, but they're just off. You come in, dearie, and sit down and rest yourself, and take that rucksack off your back. You look properly tired, as if you'd walked all the way from Scotland."

"I came by lorry," Barbary explained, following Mrs. Cox into the kitchen, where the bit of company, cheerful with supper but a trifle embarrassed at meeting one of the family, was making ready to depart.

"Three lorries, I came by," Barbary explained when they were gone. "The last one put me down at King's Cross, so I finished in a bus."

"Do you mean to tell me you drove all through last night and to-day with those lorry men? That's not what your Pa would like, which is only reasonable, in a girl of your age. They make very free, those men. Did they make free with you, love? Here, you eat up this nice bit of pie."

"No," said Barbary. "Not really free. I gave them some money instead."

Obligations, she recognised, had to be repaid.

"You gave them some money! Well, you were lucky they didn't rob you of all you had. People to-day, they've grown so independent, they stick at nothing, and more particularly in those lorries, they say. Weren't you scared?"

"No. They were nice men. They let me sleep on rugs and gave me sandwiches. The first lot were Glasgow men, and talked like Jock. They were going to Carlisle. In the morning we got coffee at a stall. The next lorry went to Scotch Corner. The driver sold petrol to garages all the way, for the black market, and got lots of money for it. It's a nice way of travelling, I shall do it again."

"Well, love, that's as may be. Young ladies should be careful, as your Pa will tell you. Which you, being reared abroad as you may say, perhaps found things different there, though they say in France you can't be too careful, as I dare say your dear Ma has often told you."

"No, I don't think she has," said Barbary; and Mrs. Cox, on second thoughts, agreed that it was improbable; after all, Barbary's dear Ma had herself never been too careful, either in France or England, nor even, many would say, careful enough.

" That reminds me, love. I must phone your Pa as I promised."

" Must you? " Barbary was reluctant that this should be done. But Mrs. Cox knew her duty; also, she enjoyed a long-distance chat with her employer and giving him news, even if it was only good news.

She came back after ten minutes.

" Your Pa's coming down. Day after to-morrow he'll be here, early. To take you back to Scotland, I shouldn't be surprised."

Barbary, munching an apple, considered this.

" Well, I'm not going back. I don't really like it there much."

" Why ever not, love? With all your cousins there to play with, and all those nice amusements. I'm sure it must be a lovely place for you, after London." And better for me too, thought Mrs. Cox, than having you about the house here, when I'm supposed to be having my time to myself and pleasing myself who comes in and out. The family has no call to come creeping back when it's on holiday, even if it *is* only Miss Barbary.

" I'd rather be here," was all that Barbary gave for explanation. " I won't be any trouble. I'll be out nearly all the time."

" Well," said Mrs. Cox, briskly clearing away, " we shall see what your Pa says. And now the sheets for your bed will want airing, I suppose."

" Oh, no, they won't, they'll be quite all right. I shall go to bed now, I'm so sleepy."

* 18 *

THE maze of little streets threading through the wilderness, the broken walls, the great pits with their dense
forests of bracken and bramble, golden ragwort and
coltsfoot, fennel and· foxglove and vetch, all the wild
rambling shrubs that spring from ruin, the vaults and
cellars and deep caves, the wrecked guild halls that had
belonged to saddlers, merchant tailors, haberdashers,
waxchandlers, barbers, brewers, coopers and coachmakers,
all the ancient city fraternities, the broken office stairways that spiralled steeply past empty doorways and
rubbled closets into the sky, empty shells of churches with
their towers still strangely spiring above the wilderness,
their empty window arches where green boughs pushed
in, their broken pavement floors—St. Vedast's, St. Alban's,
St. Anne's and St. Agnes', St. Giles Cripplegate, its tower
high above the rest, the ghosts of churches burnt in an
earlier fire, St. Olave's and St. John Zachary's, haunting the
green-flowered churchyards that bore their names, the
ghosts of taverns where merchants and clerks had drunk,
of restaurants where they had eaten—all this scarred and
haunted green and stone and brambled wilderness lying
under the August sun, a-hum with insects and astir with

secret, darting, burrowing life, received the returned traveller into its dwellings with a wrecked, indifferent calm. Here, its cliffs and chasms and caves seemed to say, is your home; here you belong; you cannot get away, you do not wish to get away, for this is the maquis that lies about the margins of the wrecked world, and here your feet are set; here you find the irremediable barbarism that comes up from the depth of the earth, and that you have known elsewhere. " Where are the roots that clutch, what branches grow, out of this stony rubbish? Son of man, you cannot say, or guess. . . ." But you can say, you can guess, that it is you yourself, your own roots, that clutch the stony rubbish, the branches of your own being that grow from it and from nowhere else.

Barbary called for Raoul in the morning; they spent the day together about London; Barbary had money in her purse; they lived well and went to a cinema in the evening. They spent the afternoon in the ruins; Barbary did a painting of Addle Street and the jungle that grew where Brewers' Hall had stood; then she and Raoul re-decorated the walls of their room in Somerset Chambers, which some *sales types* had scribbled over with most of the words that printers may not set. Raoul replaced these with a few equivalent French ones, out of patriotism, but most of the space they covered with paintings of the Last Judgment and souls in hell, such as churches have.

" I think," said Barbary, when they had finished, " we had better paint the church walls too. Anyhow, the altar end. It probably had a *jugement dernier* once, before it was bombed. We'll begin it to-morrow."

Then she remembered that to-morrow her father was coming from Scotland. I shan't go back, she thought, I shan't go back.

* *19* *

S IR GULLIVER arrived at his house at nine o'clock next
morning, cross on account of the night journey, of
having his holiday broken like this, of losing four days'
fishing, and of having a daughter who behaved as Barbary
behaved.

He met her in the hall as he came in; she had a satchel
slung from her shoulder, full of painting things and food,
and seemed about to go out.

"Oh, hallo," she said, encountering her parent in the
hall.

"Well," he returned, rather grimly. "As I have come
from Scotland entirely to see you, I hope you aren't
intending to go out just now. I am going to have a bath;
I want to talk to you in an hour."

Barbary said: "All right," and went out to feed the
birds in the embankment gardens. She felt gloomy; her
father was cold and annoyed. Did he know about the
fifteen pounds? Could she be sent to prison for it? She
would have liked to go out for the day into the ruins;
but he would only wait till she came back. She returned
to the house, fidgeting uneasily about till he came downstairs and summoned her to his study: she sat facing him,

131

frightened yet stubborn, like a child expecting a beating.

"Now, my dear Barbary," he began, in his cold, sharp, precise lawyer's voice, "I shall be glad if you will explain your behaviour."

She said nothing, fiddling with the strap of her satchel and looking out of the window at the chimneys opposite. After waiting for a moment, he went on: "What made you leave Arshaig in that way, without a word to anyone? For all we knew, you might have had an accident on the moors. But for the chance of someone having noticed you on Ardrishaig pier, we should have had to search for you all night. Now, in the first place what made you go so suddenly, and in the second why did you leave no message? . . . Barbary, I want an answer, please."

Her mind flinched at the familiar words. I want an answer; I mean to have an answer; you had better speak at once, before we make you. We can make you speak, you know. She did know, and spoke.

"I didn't like it there. I wanted to come away."

"Why? Were you unhappy there? Or had anything special happened?"

She frowned, picking at the satchel strap.

"Uncle Angus asked me things."

"What kind of things?"

"Oh . . . about France and things. . . . I didn't want to talk about it; I thought he'd make me."

"I see. . . . Do you mean about your mother, and your life with her?"

"Partly. And about the maquis, and the Germans, and what we did. Lots of things. I didn't want to talk about

132

it. I won't." Her voice rose shrilly. I *won't* talk,
I won't, I won't ; dumb refusal armed itself behind her
closed lips.

Her father's eyes, searching the dumb, closed face,
became more gentle.

"Very well, my dear child. There's no reason whatever
why you should. Your uncle thought it might help you.
You should have told him you didn't wish to, not just run
away like that. It was rather bad-mannered and silly and
childish, wasn't it ? "

Barbary said nothing.

"There's another thing," Sir Gulliver went on. "Your
uncle thought you might have taken some money—fifteen
pounds, in fact—from a bureau drawer, for your journey.
Did you ? "

"No," she replied, thinking, what a silly question, as if
anyone would say they had.

He perceived that she spoke without conviction and
without truth.

"You're lying, aren't you," he said. "Please don't. I
think you took the money : I can only hope you meant
to pay it back. But it was, of course, stealing. Do you
often steal ? "

"Not very," said Barbary. "Only when I need to."

"I see. You and your friends used to steal in France, I
take it. Did your mother know ? "

Had her mother known ? Barbary could not remember ;
perhaps she had, perhaps she hadn't. Perhaps she hadn't
cared.

"I don't know," she said. "I expect so. We all stole from

133

the Germans and from the collabos, to get things for the
Resistance. They steal here too, don't they?"

"They do," Sir Gulliver dryly agreed. "But it's something
rather new for people brought up like you to steal.
That's come on since the war, I think."

His own words echoed in his ears with a note of mockery.
Brought up like you. Come to think of it, how *had* his
daughter been brought up?

"Stealing and lying." Meditatively he turned the distasteful
words over. "Odd, how prevalent they have
become. It's distressing to find that my own daughter has
joined the criminal classes. I hope you aren't intending to
continue in the career. Are you?"

"No," said Barbary. "Not really."

"*Not really.* I see." He glanced aside, with irony, at the
jury. "That's most interesting, if a trifle ambiguous. I
presume you mean, not until the next occasion when you
need a little ready cash. . . . By the way, how much have
you left of the sum you took?"

"I don't know." She thrust her hand into her pocket
and drew out a purse. "There are some notes here. I
spent some on the journey, and some yesterday, doing
things. I think there are nine pounds left, besides some silver
and pennies and four threepennies."

He took the purse, counted the notes and the coins,
folded the notes into his notecase, and emptied most of the
coins into his purse. Barbary watched him gloomily,
perceiving that she was to have nothing of importance back,
though it was hers.

"I shall, of course, return the fifteen pounds immediately.

What you have spent will be stopped from your allowance, which will be reduced from a pound a week to ten shillings till it is made up. You will also write a letter to your aunt, apologising for taking it, as you won't be seeing her for the present. I don't propose to take you back to Scotland; obviously you would be in a difficult position there now, and they might not care to have you."

"I don't want to go back," said Barbary, sulkily. "I want to stay here."

"Indeed? How do you propose to spend your time here?"

"Painting."

This seemed to Sir Gulliver the second sensible thing she had said; the first was that she had not wanted to tell her Uncle Angus about her life. He looked at her more kindly.

"Well, that seems not a bad idea. You could, I suppose, stay here with Mrs. Cox, though I'm not sure that it is quite fair on her to give her the responsibility and trouble. An alternative plan might be for you to go to the Isle of Wight and stay with David and his nurse."

Barbary, who did not like David or his nurse, shook her head.

"I shouldn't like that. I'd rather be here."

"Very well. I'm afraid you'll have rather a dull time, but that's your own affair. It's a pity you couldn't manage to get on at Arshaig. You know, my dear child, you'll have to learn sometime to fit into the society about you. You realise that, don't you?"

Barbary wondered what society he meant. Perhaps really

she fitted into none. Fear and desolation crept like a cold wind in her stomach.

" How much longer am I staying ? " she asked, in a small, unhopeful voice.

" Staying ? Staying where ? "

" Here. In England. When do I go home ? "

He was annoyed, rather stung.

" This is your home," he returned. " If you mean, when shall you visit your mother in France again, I can't give you a precise date. You were there for some years; now, possibly, you will be here for some years. Your mother hasn't proposed that you should go back to her for the present, and I think it best that you should stay here, learning to paint, if that's what you want to do, and learning to behave like a properly brought up young woman."

He had not been prepared for the effect of his words. His daughter was staring at him with startled eyes, her mouth open and quivering, her hands clenched together on her knees.

" No," she cried. " Oh, *no*! Not for some years. . . . Oh, *please*. . . ."

He looked at her, balanced between displeasure and compassion.

" You want to see your mother," he said gently, cold but reasonable. " I understand that. And I didn't mean that you shouldn't visit her for short times—unless she should come to England to see you. What I meant was that you will not make your home with her in France. Perhaps you are aware that I am your legal guardian, till you are of age. So I am afraid you must make the best of

136

the situation, disagreeable as it seems to be to you. And, while we are on the subject of your future, I must ask you to be as little troublesome as you can to Pamela, during these next months. I don't want her worried and upset. If you can make friends with her, so much the better; if you can't, at least try to behave civilly and not to annoy her."

"She doesn't like me living here," Barbary muttered; she was trying not to cry, her face bent down.

"It is," said Sir Gulliver, frowning, "a pity to talk like that; it only underlines the elements in a situation that are better ignored. The situation obviously can't be easy; it is for you and Pamela to make the best of it. A little effort may be necessary, but it should be made. Civilised people can manage to get on together, even when not naturally particularly compatible."

Civilised. Odd word, it did not seem here to apply: Barbary glanced at it with uninterested eyes. Her lack of response goaded her civilised parent to his sharp final word.

"And, anyhow," he added, "I must insist that you don't steal."

She muttered: "All right," and he got up.

"Well, that's all, I think. I'm going back by the evening train. I shan't be at home for lunch, or in the afternoon, so I may not see you before I go. If not, good-bye for the present. I'm sorry not to have you with us at Arshaig; if you had given it a chance I think you would have got to enjoy the place. It was really a little stupid of you, wasn't it. Next summer perhaps you can try it again, if they invite you."

At the words " next summer," at the thought of the autumn, winter, spring, that stretched themselves drearily ahead before that, at the memory of other summers, other autumns, winters, springs, Barbary broke into tears. Next summer would at last arrive, bringing with it what? A possible invitation to Arshaig. She cried, bent over the back of her chair, her face in her arms.

At the sight of his child so forlorn and distressed, Sir Gulliver's hurt reserve melted. He bent over her, his arm about her heaving shoulders.

" My poor child. I hate to leave you like this. Yes, I know how you miss your mother. So do I. I promise you shall see her again before long. Meanwhile, will you try to be happy with me here? You must believe me it's the best way for the present. . . . Look, Barbary: would you like it if you and I went away together somewhere now? "

She stopped crying, and looked up at him.

" To Collioure? " she questioned, hope struggling with doubt in her shaking voice. " To mummy? "

" No, my dear. Your mother wouldn't want us. I meant somewhere in the country, where I would fish and you could bathe, or ride, or do what you liked. I'd like to have you with me. It's time you and I got to know each other better, don't you think? I like to have a daughter as well as a son. Well, what do you say? Shall we go off for a fortnight together? "

" Oh, please do send for mummy to come too. Then it would be lovely. And please send *her* away, so that mummy can come back. Oh, please do ! "

He stood back from her; the unaccustomed caress left his voice and face.

"My dear child, you're being merely childish. You mustn't say things like that. Your mother and I ended our marriage, by her desire. I am now married to someone else. The last thing your mother would wish is to come back to me, even if it were possible. She married someone else too, you know."

"He's dead, he's dead, he's dead," she cried, and her voice fell to a whisper. "He was drowned." On the desolate, engulfing word she gave a shuddering sob.

"I know." He had not realised before how much she grieved for this. "Forget these past unhappy things, Barbary; life goes on, you know. Will you come away with me?"

She shook her head. "I'd rather stay here, please."

"Very well. I'm sorry you won't come. Good-bye, then." He kissed her gently; but aloofness had returned with the rebuff. He left her without more words.

He would, he told himself, try again later on. He had hoped, out of the embittering and humiliating wreckage of his first marriage, to have salvaged a son and a daughter. He wondered now if it was to be, after all, only a son; whether the daughter would eventually qualify as salvage, or would remain drifting with the wreckage, drifting beyond his reach, enspelled by an enchantress from whom no one ever broke quite free.

* 20 *

OFTEN in the evenings the Abbé Dinant would walk over to the Villa Fraises and sit with Helen and her son in the aromatic, sun-drenched garden. He insisted that they talked English with him, since he desired to practise himself in this peculiar tongue. Occasionally Lucien Michel would be there from Toulouse, and then they spoke French. Lucien had told Helen that he really could not absent himself from her society for the whole summer; her intruding son, he said, must put up with the occasional company of his mother's closest friend.

" A charming boy," he admitted. " Civilised, agreeable, intelligent, elegantly mannered. Assuredly, my dear, too much of the world to disapprove. I have no doubt that he is delighted that you should find consolations, and would not wish you to be alone."

So, after the first week of Richie's stay, Helen had consented, only insisting on an experimental visit to see how they got on. They got on well, it seemed; Lucien laid himself out to be agreeable, and Richie to be hospitable and polite; after that, Lucien came over once or twice each week, and sometimes stayed the night. When the abbé called and found him there, they were all courteously oblivious of any relationship beyond friendship, and behaved with the utmost good manners and tact.

They would sit in the warm garden, while the evening primroses opened and the frogs cawed, drinking, sometimes playing cards, more often talking. The abbé and Lucien would usually get on to the subject of France: her present disarranged and discouraged state, her chances of revival.

"We have been through too much," the abbé said with sadness. "We are beaten down, we have no longer, for the present, heart for the struggle for existence. There is bitterness and apathy and malice and revenge, and always this black market poisoning the springs of our economy. It is very bad. Who knows (except the good God) what will come of it? We have been through wars before, we have had military occupations, but we have recovered quickly; there is a formidable vitality in our people. But now even this vitality seems to have taken a wrong turn; I see it like marsh fires running without direction over a treacherous poison swamp. Work, country, family—those great ideals held before us by the old Marshal during the black years—are discredited by his disgrace, and held of little account now that those who always hated him are dominant. It is a catastrophe, that, for they are great ideals, and always when we have turned our backs on them we have deserted our true rôle."

"You are extremely right, M. l'Abbé," Lucien politely agreed. "Our workers do not work, they have been demoralised by the years of working for the enemy, or, alternately, of working against him. They dawdle and chatter of politics, while the wheels of the factories run slow. In my own factory at Toulouse, it is the managers who work; the workmen take their ease and hanker after the millenium to which they had looked forward after victory, but which does not arrive."

" One understands so well," said Helen, languidly teasing a small green lizard cupped in her hand, " the desire not to work; indeed, I share it to the full. As to one's country, why should one feel any more interest in its welfare than in that of other countries? And as to the family, I have never understood how that fits in with the other ideals—or, indeed, why it should be an ideal at all. A group of closely related persons living under one roof; it is a convenience, often a necessity, sometimes a pleasure, sometimes the reverse; but who first exalted it as admirable, an almost religious ideal? "

" My dear Madame, not *almost*. It *is* a religious ideal." The abbé spoke dryly, and did not add anything about the Holy Family at Nazareth, for he never talked in such a manner to his worldly, unbelieving friends.

Helen smiled at him with affection; she was fond of the abbé and appreciated his reserves, and knew that he cherished a distant hope that one day she might suffer conversion. Meanwhile he was a good, entertaining and amiable friend, and looked on her vagaries with a polite reticence which she did not mistake for acquiescence.

Lucien, a little impatient when the conversation took a religious turn, brought it back to earth with, "We shall never make progress until we stop these everlasting quarrels and revenges, the Resistance hunting down collaborators, the collabos too busy vindicating themselves to get on with

their business, everyone jealous and suspicious of everyone
else, and those damned conceited workmen accusing their
employers of having surrendered to the Boches out of class
fear. One gets sick of such ignorant, arrogant talk, in which
they're encouraged by all the malicious little left-wing
intellectuals. In Toulouse, outrages and violent attacks
occur daily; no one is safe, no one is content, nothing is
efficient. The police can't cope with the crimes that rage
about the town."

Richie said that Toulouse sounded extremely like
London.

"And yet in London," Lucien gloomily pointed out,
"you have had no Resistance, no maquis, no foreign
occupation, no defeat."

Richie said that London could apparently manage an
adequate quota of crime without these incentives.

"A large number of the inhabitants of both countries,"
said the abbé, solving the problem with ease, "have turned
from God. One needs no more; it is enough."

He offered his snuff box to both gentlemen; Richie
took a pinch, feeling like a man of the world.

"And yet," the abbé went on, "we have also, together
with the decline in faith, a considerable return to it. During
the occupation, the churches were full; the congregations
have since a little dwindled, but still are good. Is that so
in England too?"

"Oh, I don't think so," Richie said. "Not *good*. And
those that do go to church often steal handbags there, I'm
afraid. It is better not to go, or to go and steal handbags,
should you say?"

"Certainly the latter," the abbé told him. "For those who steal in church can seek forgiveness at once, but those who pass by the doors without entering do not even know their need of repentance. To sin in our Father's house, that, though sacrilege, has its own blessedness. To stray in the wilderness outside, that is to be lost indeed. And that, alas, is what so many of the sons and daughters of the Resistance are now doing. . . . You were very wise, Madame, to send your young daughter and your stepson away from this region, where they had, I know, some undesirable friends. I hope your daughter is happy in England?"

"I hope so," Helen answered, letting the lizard run up and down her arm. "In any case, she is better there. She is at the Slade school of art. I think she has a little talent."

"And when does she visit you again here?"

"Not this year. She mustn't be continually interrupted in her life."

And nor, the abbé reflected, must you. Yet, my dear friend, I could wish you had her here, for your own sake, though not for hers.

He glanced covertly at the handsome, worldly, pleasant face of Lucien, to see how *he* regarded the contingency of a visit from Barbary; it was apparent to him that Lucien, unconcerned, saw no early prospect of it. As to the son, he was bland and civil and gay, and obviously was causing no trouble, perhaps feeling none. Daughters, *jeunes filles*, are a different affair altogether, even daughters as *farouche*, as wild, as *peu demoiselle*, as the little Barbary.

It occurred to the abbé, not for the first time, that he would like to talk alone with Richie. He rose to go.

" I have," he said, " a visit to make a mile away. I am wondering if Monsieur Richie would give me the pleasure of walking with me a short way ? "

Richie by all means would give the abbé and himself this pleasure.

* *21* *

THEY set off up the hill behind the villa, along a stony
track between vineyards. The evening sunshine lay
warmly on the dry land; in the trees the cicadas cawed
like frogs. People came down the path on bicycles, going
into Collioure; they saluted the abbé as they passed,
speaking the Spanish French of Roussillon; many were
as dark as Spaniards.

"My well-loved compatriots," the abbé said to Richie.
"They are my people; I was born at Perpignan, and grew
up talking Catalan French. I have the well-being of these
people in my heart. It has fallen sadly low during the past
years. Defeat, occupation by a brutal enemy, these are
good for no one. Neither is violent resistance good, nor
collaboration. Worst of all is the anger and hate between
those two sections of people. There is much lawless
wickedness in this district now, and many marauders come
over the mountains from Spain. Everything is deranged;
morality, discipline, chastity. There is much Communism
and Atheism. One would wish that those who have had
more advantages than these poor people would set them a
better example. Laxity among the rich encourages im-
morality among the poor, isn't it so?"

146

" I don't know. It seems possible."

" It is certain. Therefore, the rich should try to avoid offence. Unfortunately they don't always do so."

" No, they don't, do they? After all, it is not to be expected that they should, since the rich too, are human."

" Alas, yes. Perhaps if they did but know the harm they do, they would think twice about it. Sin in high places is a veritable tragedy. Those who live loosely and flout the laws of God in public are responsible for much. . . . You love your mother, Monsieur Richie? "

Richie had faintly coloured during this speech. " Naturally," he agreed.

" Then you will forgive me if I appeal to you to use with her your influence as a son, in a matter which I will not name, but which you will readily guess. I regret if I give you pain, but the affair is yet another scandal in a country which has already too many. One thinks, too, of the sin against the poor wife in Toulouse. I have not spoken to Madame on this subject; I have not ventured, though we are excellent friends. She has such great and valuable gifts that it gives me pain to see her descending to a lower level. It was bad enough when she lived with Maurice Michel, having a husband in England, and became a divorced woman. But this present affair gives more scandal, for it is not a year since poor Maurice died, and now she receives his cousin, who has a wife. He lived at the Fraises all the summer. All the neighbourhood is aware of it. As her son, Monsieur Richie, can you use your influence? "

" No," Richie said. " I have no influence. And if I had

I should not use it to try and alter my mother's way of life. It's not my business, how she chooses to live."

The abbé sighed. He had done his best and failed.

" I regret that you see it like that. For it seems to me that it is very much your business, as a loving son. If you were a Catholic, you would feel it to be so, I think."

" Possibly." If ever I become a Catholic, Richie thought, perhaps I shall. What a nuisance mother would find me. Perhaps I should go on like Hamlet, mother go not to his bed, assume a virtue if you have it not. . . . But I don't think I shall be a Catholic. I admire the abbé, but how he embarrasses me. I hope he will soon come to the house he is to visit, for our conversation seems now over, and it is my fault.

At the next turning the abbé left him. " Here," he said, " is my way." He extended his snuff box to Richie. " You will forgive me if I have given you pain."

" Not at all." Richie took a pinch; with mutual unspoken apologies they parted.

Richie climbed on up the hill path, which now twisted among cork-oak woods in the deepening twilight. Up the forested slope it wound, up the Pyrenean foothills towards Spain. It would soon leave the vineyards, the tilled lands, the pastures of France; it would twist through barren wildness, it would climb into desolation, it would meet Spain. The menace of Spain crept down the mountains: this was Roussillon, ancient home of wild Visigoths fleeing over the mountains from Saracens, ancient fief of Barcelona counts, later a province of the kings of Aragon, a prey to Spanish armies, to French invaders, to the trampling of the nations and the kings at war. It was still more Spanish than French; its swarthy peasants talked Catalan, smuggled contraband over the mountain passes, had brothers, cousins, parents, sons, across the frontier.

The cool evening wind rustled in the cork forest, crept about the thymey maquis; the sea, drained of light, was a wash of blue shadow, sparked by the lights of fishing boats putting out for the night's catch. Collioure glimmered in its cove, shut by the Templars' fortress on its northern jut of rock.

The peace that shrouded land and sea was a mask, lying thinly over terror, over hate, over cruel deeds done. Barbarism prowled and padded, lurking in the hot sunshine, in the warm scents of the maquis, in the deep shadows of the forest. Visigoths, Franks, Catalans, Spanish, French, Germans, Anglo-American armies, savageries without number, the Gestapo torturing captured French patriots, rounding up fleeing Jews, the Resistance murdering, derailing trains full of people, lurking in the shadows to kill, collaborators betraying Jews and escaped prisoners, working together with the victors, being in their turn killed and mauled, hunted down by mobs hot with rage; everywhere cruelty, everywhere vengeance, everywhere the barbarian on the march.

Richie, himself trapped into barbarism for three long, unbelievable years, shrank back from it, reacted towards gentleness, towards bland tolerance, towards an excessive civility. The rich elegances of life, now so little probable, the fine decoration, the exquisite glow of colour and grace of structure, the beauty that wealth and knowledge can

bring, the fineness, the ivory tower of aristocratic culture,
that war and peace had undermined, had set tottering, had
all but brought down with a crash, to replace by pre-fabs
for the multitude, by a thin, weak, tainted mass culture—
it was towards these obsolescent things that Richie
nostalgically turned, pursuing their light retreating steps
as one chases beloved ghosts. In this pursuit he was im-
pelled sometimes beyond his reasoning self, to grasp at the
rich, trailing panoplies, the swinging censors, of churches
from whose creeds and uses he was alien, because at least
they embodied some continuance, some tradition; while
cities and buildings, lovely emblems of history, fell
shattered, or lost shape and line in a sprawl of common
mass newness, while pastoral beauty was overrun and spoilt,
while ancient communities were engulfed in the gaping
maw of the beast of prey, and Europe dissolved into
wavering anonyminities, bitter of tongue, servile of deed,
faint of heart, always treading the frail plank over the
abyss, rotten-ripe for destruction, turning a slanting,
doomed eye on death that waited round the corner—
during all this frightening evanescence and dissolution the
historic churches kept their strange courses, kept their
improbable, incommunicable secret, linking the dim past
with the disrupted present and intimidating future, frail,
tough chain of legend, myth, and mystery, stronghold of
reaction and preserved values. When Richie said, to himself
or others, perhaps I shall be a Catholic, he reached towards
this stronghold against which it was possible that the gates
of hell might not prevail, though they clanged with their
iron clamour on all else. But when he envisaged saying

this to his sceptical, ironic father, or to his detached, amused mother, what he had from them in his blood surged up like the white corpuscles that run to cure a wound, and he smiled back in their faces, reassuring them. Anglican, then, he compromised, and that would go better with his father, suggesting to him college chapels, good glass windows, Byrd anthems, Gothic cathedrals, the Temple church, the benchers at lunch on Sundays at Lincoln's Inn; to his mother, however, it would all be one; though she would no doubt agree that in the latter church there was less to believe.

His mother. When did people—women—outgrow love affairs? Fifty? Sixty? There would be several years yet of enjoyment for her, of scandal for Collioure and the abbé, and of embarrassment for him. She was so beautiful still, and took pleasure as it came her way, selective but casual, as if it did not really matter very much but one might as well have it.

She was planning an exploration of the Greek islands next spring; she had asked him to go with her; Lucien's business, it seemed, would make it difficult for him to spare the time. If neither her lover nor her son could go, she would pick up someone else, or be as happy alone. She had to live that way, carelessly attached, fundamentally detached: to try to interfere with her would be like trying to deflect a force of nature from its course. In the end, it might be Barbary who would be taken to Greece; perhaps Barbary and Richie together; if Barbary was forgiven by then (the word came oddly into his mind: forgiven for what?).

The mountain wind from Spain rustled harshly in the forest; herds of lean pigs trampled by. Richie descended the hill quickly, seeking reassurance in the tilled olive groves and vineyards of France. Savagery waited so close on the margins of life; one day it would engulf all: yet another civilisation would go down into darkness, so historians and philosophers said, to join *les autres*, those sunk civilisations of past ages which can be dimly seen, magnificent wrecks, lying fathoms deep in the seas of time. No civilisation had lasted more than a few thousand years; this present one, called western culture, had had its day and was due for wreckage, due for drowning, while the next struggled inchoate in the womb of the ensuing chaos, till slowly it too would take shape and have its day. That day was unimaginable; it would be what it would be; but already the margins of the present broke crumbling and dissolved before the invading chaos that pressed on, We haven't finished, Richie protested, we have scarcely begun, give us a little more time for beauty. O, I love long life better than figs. But beauty vanishes, beauty passes, and he saw only her receding back, menaced and to die.

The lean pigs scuffled and rooted in the dark forest behind him; the savage swine who trampled the pearls and passed snorting on their way.

Richie came down on to the path that led to the Fraises; through the aromatic garden, through the dark boughs of the tall orange and lemon trees that rose above the pink garden walls, lights shone from the tall open-shuttered windows. Lucien was still there; he would spend the night. Probably Helen would now be upstairs, saying good night to Roland.

Richie went in. Lucien sat on the veranda drinking and keeping off the mosquitoes with his cigar.

"Well," he said, "so you conducted our good abbé on his way. He had, no doubt, much to say."

"Well," said Richie, sitting down and pouring himself a drink, "not so much. Chiefly about the wicked state of the world, and more particularly of France."

"And most particularly, perhaps, of the Perpignan district of Roussillon."

"More or less."

Lucien, through drifts of blue smoke, watched the young man's face, pale, fine-featured, bland, with its raised ironic brows and thin-lipped mouth, as he lay back in the long chair, glass in hand. He liked the boy, civil and gentle and coolly aloof, but could not read his mind. Helen said he was like his father, the English lawyer, but had more sympathy, more tolerance, more imagination, probably less moral uprightness. Helen said he did not mind their association, and was neither disapproving, jealous nor hurt, but went his own way, politely leaving her to hers. Lucien always exerted himself to entertain and interest Richie, and believed that he succeeded. Richie, glancing at him through the half-lit dusk, saw a square, handsome olive face, dark, thick brows, a well-curved, sensual mouth, crisp dark hair touched with grey, scarcely yet receding, a firmly built broadish body, thick strong hands, made to grasp a wheel and keep a large car steady on the road at excessive speeds. He thought what a handsome pair they

made, Lucien and his mother, and how the abbé had no
chance at all with them.

Morality—what was it? Did any of them know? The
wife in Toulouse? Did any of them care? Perhaps she
had her own consolations. Richie, a sympathetic young
man, hoped so. For the rest, he had no Œdipus complex,
and was no more jealous of the man his mother loved
than of the woman to whom his father was married.
Let them both, by all means, be happy, not lonely ;
it relieved their children from a responsibility neither
was well qualified to bear. Parents are untamed, excessive, potentially troublesome creatures; charming to
be with for a time, in the main they must lead their own
lives, independent and self-employed, with companions of
their own age and selection, not with those planted on
them by the inscrutable and capricious workings of nature
and divided from them by a gulf of years. That was where
Barbary, so inexperienced in life, went wrong: her heart
was fixed on one of these capricious wild pets, and could
not disentangle. Parents, unfortunately, sometimes had
charm, and held sons and daughters (or was it only daughters,
those unbalanced, prodigal beings?) in a net, like leaping
fishes gasping in an alien air. Richie, wiser, never gasped;
he pursued his own way, or hoped to, on an even, if
uncertain keel.

"The abbé," Lucien went on, "has the concern with
morals proper to his profession."

His voice turned up on the last words, *son métier*, as if he
asked a question.

"Perfectly," Richie answered. "It is very right of
154

him." The bland inexpressiveness of his face and voice reassured Lucien.

"But a man of good sense," he added, changing the subject. "During the occupation he did his best to keep the peace, and preached against the violence of the hot-heads of the Resistance, as the poor old Marshal bade him. Yet a good patriot all the same, and never betrayed a soul to Vichy or the Germans; no, not so much as one Jew. Since the liberation he has protected many from mob vengeance. In these days, as before, his chief foe is Communism; he sees it as the devil, and as France's first enemy, and he is right. It is working to destroy France and all she stands for; if it conquers, our civilisation will go under. In England you have less of that danger, I believe." And also, he believed, less of civilisation.

"Much less," Richie agreed. "Our Communists are regarded as something of a joke. Tiresome, of course, and with too much influence in the Trades Unions. But not a great force, like yours."

"What of those young intellectuals, university students, and so on, who were so formidably to the Left before the war?"

"I don't know—I think many of them have been cured by Moscow. Anyhow, they wouldn't be so young still, I suppose? I don't think I actually know any Communists. More reactionaries, I think."

"Ah, reactionaries. I myself am a reactionary." Lucien settled himself comfortably back in his chair. With re-actionaries he felt relaxed, relieved, at home; they were sensible types, and good for business.

" As to your mother, my dear, I, and indeed she, have no idea what her politics are."

" I don't think she has any."

Helen came out on to the veranda.

" My dear Lucien, I have told you before—I am an old-English whig. Like my volatile ancestor, Charles James Fox. Thank you, Richie; yes, a vermouth and gin."

" A reactionary, then," Richie said, " like us. Here's to us." He raised his glass to a dim, improbable future, in which reactionaries would sit cosily in deep chairs, enjoying their ease, undisturbed by the hoarse, menacing babble of intruding mobs, or by the platitudes of their rulers who, though, owing to their official positions, they sometimes walked with kings, still kept the all too common touch.

" And if M. the Abbé were with us," said Lucien, " he would join in the toast."

The splashing of the wind-raised sea broke through the fragrant evening, as the cool breeze roved about. From the shore and the town came a medley of harsh Roussillon voices, raised in dispute.

" The canaille who quarrel among themselves," Lucien remarked, quite pleasantly, for he liked people. " They sound like the croaking of the frogs in the pond."

Richie thought, this is perhaps the way the French noblesse sat and talked just before the Revolution: and look what happened to *them*.

" These damned gnats," Helen said. " I am going in. A game of piquet before dinner, Lucien? Richie? "

It was Richie who played, for Lucien had discouraging business papers to read.

* 22 *

BARBARY and Raoul picked up two bicycles in an alley off Cheapside one Sunday, rode them to Gresham Street, and hid them in one of the deep caves of Haberdashers' Hall.

"We will put them back in the same street after a few days," Barbary said, having been bidden by her father not to steal.

"Why?" asked Raoul. "That would be silly. They will be very useful to us. We were fortunate to find them unguarded and unlocked. We will keep them, and ride about London."

"They might be recognised," Barbary doubtfully suggested; but he shrugged his shoulders.

"Little probable, among so many machines, so many people. If they are, we will say that we found them abandoned and took charge of them. It is the truth."

"Yes," Barbary agreed. "So it is."

They stood together in the tall, tangled jungle of Haberdashers' Hall, knee-deep in shrubs and bracken and fireweed, outside the deep door that led to the cave where the bicycles had been thrust. Round them the bees buzzed and hummed, like merchants chaffering.

157

" I find it very English, this city," Raoul said, using the English word. " A great habitation of merchants, that is what it was."

The innocent cunning of the merchants bumbled about them in the warm, sleepy afternoon. What careful, crafty affairs had they transacted in the Hall of the Haberdashers, in that of the Goldsmiths and of the Waxchandlers across the road, at the wholesale umbrella manufacturers whose wrecked foundations crumbled on the corner, in the office of Mr. Perara on the first floor of the shell of flats in Addle Street? Had they pledged each other in good wine at the Coopers' Arms, which only a board now marked? Had they, on Sunday mornings, attended Divine Service at St. Anne's and St. Agnes' among the fig-trees, at St. Alban's, at St. Giles's, at St. Vedast's which had been St. Foster's, and, long ago, at the parish church of St. Olave in Silver Street, " a small thing," perished long since? Had they drunk from dairymaids' pails in Milk Street (" so called of milk sold there "), counted their shillings in Silver Street (" I think of silversmiths dwelling there "), swindled the peers who dwelt in Noble Street, that alley twisting through the wilderness of weeds, bought tables (as Pepys did) from the joiners in Wood Street, and courted in Love Lane (" so called of wantons")? What orgies, what cheepings, what market-shaking deals had been conducted in those jungled alleys and caves behind those broken, gaping, painted doors? What gems, what wines, what barley and what oil, had been stored in those labyrinthine mazes of cellars, where now rats and rabbits scuttered and gnawed? Cellars so solid, on foundations so deep dug,

that two great fires and more, storming over them, had yet
left their bases set. "We saw the fire grow . . . in corners
and upon steeples, and between churches and houses, as far
as we could see up the hill of the city, in a most horrid
malicious bloody flame, not like the fine flame of an ordinary fire. . . . The churches, houses, and all on fire and
flaming at once; and a horrid noise the flames made, and
the cracking of houses at their ruin. . . ."

Still the ghosts of the centuries-old merchant cunning
crept and murmured among weeds and broken stones,
flitted like bats about dust-heaped, gaping rooms. But their
companion ghosts, ghosts of an ancient probity, honourable
and mercantile and proud and tough, that had lived side by
side with cunning in the stone ways, and in the great
blocks of warehouses and offices and halls, had deserted and
fled without trace, leaving their broken dwellings to the
creeping jungle and the crafty shades.

Barbary, sitting presently on the top floor of a high
ladder of offices in Addle Street ("the reason of which
name I know not, for at this present it is replenished with
fair buildings on both sides"), painted on postcards the
rambling ruins to the west, where Silver Street ran through
a golden and green and purple wilderness, past St. Olave's
churchyard, past the halls of Parish Clerks and Coachmakers, past the Coopers' Arms to Noble Street and tiny
Monkwell Street that ran north to Cripplegate. She painted
rapidly, impressionistically: out of the flowering jungle
shells of towered churches sprang, shells of flats soared sky-
ward on twisting stairs, staring empty-eyed at desolation.
She could sell all her postcards at a shilling each, standing

outside the café in Fore Street, where a few people strolled
by and paused to look. She and Raoul had become known
figures to the few who came and went in those ruined streets;
on week days workmen busy excavating would greet them,
and passing policemen would eye them without malice, or
more suspicion than policemen must necessarily entertain
for juvenile loiterers. They would enter the narrow strip
of St. Giles's churchyard and eat their lunch or tea seated
on the flat tomb of Sir William Staines and his large family.
Then they would often climb through a window into the
great roofless church, and there Barbary would pace up the
aisle to the east end, kneel in devotion before the vanished
altar, and chant the Dies Irae. Raoul, finding this a bore,
would not always enter the church; he preferred to
climb about the flat terrace of Somerset Chambers and
peer down through the great round frame of the lost east
window.

After they had acquired the bicycles, they would often
go for rides, up and down the steep streets that run from
Cheapside to the river, down Queen Street to the wharfs
—Brooks Wharf, Darkhouse Lane, Queen Hithe Stairs,
Anchor Alley, Southwark Bridge Stairs, and along the
wharfs between All Hallows Lane and London Bridge.
They joined other wharf rats, scrambling among bales and
warehouses, sneaking, when unwatched, on to barges,
climbing up and down water-lapped stairs, while the dark
and shining river swirled muddily by. Often they went
farther afield, pedalling through hideous grey suburbs, or
to Regents Park or Battersea, slipping perilously between
the rushing monsters that thundered along the streets,

imitating these in ignoring traffic lights, riding fast and
furious, crouched low over bent handles. Raoul, being
French, could go fastest; neither experienced fear. At
times they were thrown, and injured not seriously; once
Raoul's wheel was buckled; he left the machine on the
kerb and boarded a bus; in three days he had picked up
another. They had begun to believe in themselves as
pickers up; the professional crook's exhilaration of self-
confidence succeeded the amateur's apprehension, which,
long since trained out of them in France, had afflicted them
when transported to this new field of operations, whose
rules they had not learnt.

Sometimes Barbary would bring Raoul back with her
to supper. Mrs. Cox did not object to this, so long as they
talked English, so that she could keep a line on the conversation; if it was French, she did not know what they were
up to. She had a motherly feeling towards the thin, polite,
whey-faced French schoolboy who was her one-time
mistress's stepson. She refused, however, to admit Barbary's
other friends, the low types that she seemed to pick up like
fleas when out. No blandishments of these young men,
and occasional young women, concealed from her experienced eyes what they were, which was spivs. And spivs
she had no intention of admitting into the house.

"Your Pa," she said firmly to Barbary, "would *not* wish
it. And nor, which is more, would there be the right
number of spoons and forks remaining to the house, once
those sat down to a meal here. No, Miss Barbary, I know
bad characters, when I see them, however soft they speak,
and I'll say that those young men are well spoken enough

to me; but inside these doors they do not push. And you'll be wise not to let them get too familiar with you, my dear, for no good will come of that, and so your Pa would tell you."

Having reflected a little further, while she and Barbary laid the table for supper, she said, aloofly, " Deserters. That's what those young men are, if you ask me. Deserters, that left the army before they should, and have been on the run ever since. It's they deserters that commit half the crimes. They are unsafe young men, my dear, and you shouldn't go with them. By rights, I should write to your Pa. . . ."

" Oh, no, Coxy, don't bother him. I don't go with them, really—not much. And if you tell father, he might tell the police, and set them hunting for them. It wouldn't be fair. Besides, he wants to be let alone, fishing and shooting. Please, Coxy."

" Very well, my dear, I won't write for the present. I'm sure it's not my wish to upset your Pa without need. But into this house those young men do not come, and neither will good food go out of it for them. Like others, those young men can work for their bread. Or so I presume; and if they cannot, there is good reason why not, and that reason no credit to them."

Barbary thought of the discredited young men, the hunted, the hunters, the hiders, so quick, so furtive, so fugitive, like lizards poised on a rock, glancing right and left for enemies, like wild cats in the maquis, glancing up and down for prey. No, nothing was any credit to them; they had no credit in the world; all their affairs went kim-kam; but still, elusive, evasive, violent, crafty, they managed to exist.

" And I ask, Miss Barbary, that on no account will you ever *trust* those young men, for of trust they will never be deserving."

Barbary, experienced in discredited young men, had never thought of trusting any of them. Lend them something, and you never had it back; leave anything about near them, and you did not see it again. If they could derive advantage from betraying you, betray you they would; these were the simple laws of their lives, the simple, easy laws of the bad, who had not to reckon with the complication of scruples, but only with gain and loss, comfort and hardship, safety and risk. Specious and crafty as they were, the young men had no credit, no trust; they were wild cats in the maquis, sneaking into larders and streaking out again, licking the cream from their whiskers as they fled back to their lairs. Sometimes they vanished, and you did not see them again, for good reasons that were, as Mrs. Cox would say, no credit to them. Three days ago two of them had stolen from the jungle-grown cellar in Haberdashers' Hall the bicycles that had been hidden there, and had ridden them away. Next day they had looked innocent, licking the cream from their whiskers, denying knowledge of the theft. Nothing to be done about it, in that jungle world in which justice could not be invoked, in which the only safety—and how incomplete—from betrayal was the universal guilt, in which the hated enemy, pacing ominously heavily, on the jungle margins, integrated its denizens into a wary school-tie solidarity, defensive yet precarious.

"Oh, no, Coxy," Barbary said, in surprise at the
eccentric idea suggested to her. "I should never trust them.
I mean, trust them with *what*? Or to do what? There
couldn't be anything. . . ."

No, there was nothing. Not bicycles, not secrets, not
money, not help in any emergency, not life; only the
simple law of their being, to take what they could and how
they could, and to keep, if they could, out of the way of
the enemy.

23

SUNDAY morning in St. Giles's. The small portable radio (stolen by Jock and presented to Barbary) stood at the base of a pillar and played jazz. Barbary and Raoul stood before the east wall, whereon a Judgment Day painting now faintly burgeoned: God the Father, with the blessed souls smiling on his right hand, on his left the wicked damned taking off for the leap into the flames. They were pleased with this painting, which had admirable clarity of design, though, owing to the nature of the wall's surface, the colours did not stand out very distinctly. Looking up at it, Barbary sang from the torn hymn-book in her hand:

> " *With thy favoured sheep O place me,*
> *Nor among the goats abase me,*
> *But to thy right hand upraise me. . . .*"

Raoul meanwhile held out a black kitten before the phantom altar: it was their symbolic sacrificial offering; they had found it creeping about the jungle in Wax-chandlers' Hall; it mewed and struggled in Raoul's hands, as if it feared the sacrificial knife.

It was on this scene, the praying figures, the mewing

kitten, the Judgment flaring on the empty wall, the jazz blaring from the floor, that the clergyman looked through the west window, parting the branches that screened it, then climbing in and dropping to the floor. He was a clergyman of middle age; thin and grey haired, he had a lost look in his deep-set eyes, and his mouth was set in lines of pain. He walked up the church, a gaunt cassocked form; in one hand he held a prayer-book, in the other a small censer. Coming up to Barbary and Raoul he stopped, and touched Raoul on the shoulder.

"I am going to say mass," he said. "Please stop that noise," he indicated the radio by the pillar, "and put down your kitten. I want you to swing this censer. Can you swing a censer?"

"Yes, *mon père.*" Raoul had learned thurifer duties during the lifetime of his pious mother.

The clergyman lit the censer and proceeded to the east end. He gave a look at the Last Judgment, and bowed his head, as if in melancholy assent. Then, kneeling, he began to pray. His congregation had small acquaintance with the Anglican rite of Holy Communion, but they stood at attention while it was intoned, Raoul swinging the censer competently enough to release a few fragrant puffs, while Barbary nursed the kitten. Neither knew the creed in English; but they genuflected and crossed themselves when the priest did so. At the end of it he turned and walked a few steps to where the pulpit had stood; standing there, he motioned to them to be seated, and began to preach. He preached about hell.

"We are in hell now," he said, staring apprehensively

166

about him. " Hell is where I am, Lucifer and all his legions
are in me. Fire creeps on me from all sides; I am trapped
in the prison of my sins; I cannot get out, there is no
rescue possible, for I have shut myself from God in the
hell of my own making. I cannot move my limbs, I cannot
raise my hands to God, I cannot call to him from my
place of darkness. The flames press on; they will consume
my body, but my soul will live on in hell, for ever damned
for I have turned from God and he must turn from me.
O, the way's dark and horrid! I cannot see: shall I have
no company? O yes, my sins; they run before me to
fetch fire from hell. Trapped, trapped, trapped; there's no
hope.

> *And see where God*
> *Stretcheth out his arm and bends his ireful brows.*
> *Mountains and hills, come, come and fall on me,*
> *And hide me from the heavy wrath of God.*
> *O soul, be changed to little ducks and geese,*
> *And dive into the ocean, ne'er be found*
> *O I'll leap up to God! what pulls me down?*

The weight of my sins: they lie across my chest and pin
me; I cannot stir. For this is hell, hell, hell."

His voice broke strangled in his throat; shuddering, he
fell to his knees, his face in his scarred hands.

Barbary, also on her knees, was crying. It was true, then,
about hell; there was no deliverance. Raoul sat still, his
black eyes staring frightened at the clergyman, the censer
fallen from his hands to roll on the floor.

Footsteps hurried up the church from the west window;

a young clergyman appeared; approaching the kneeling priest, he laid a gentle hand on his shoulder.

" Dear Father Roger, will you come with me ? "

The priest raised a ravaged face, staring up with dazed eyes.

" I cannot come. I am held here. There is no way out of hell."

" Dear Father, it is all right. I have come to take you out, to take you home. You are rescued, saved, set free."

Silently the priest looked round him, looked up and down, raised his arms, rose to his feet.

" I can stand," he muttered. " I can move. Has God set me free from the trap of sin ? "

" Yes, dear Father, he has set you free. And now you are coming home with me. Come."

The young clergyman picked up the fallen prayer-book, then the censer.

" You mustn't," he said to Barbary, " be troubled about him." Dropping his voice, he added: " He often wanders about the ruined churches, looking for his own. His church was bombed in 1940; he was trapped in the wreckage for two days; he could scarcely move, and the flames raged round him. He hasn't, of course, been the same since. He lives in a clergy house now; we all love him, but we can't always save him from his nightmares. He thinks he's in hell and can't get out. I'm afraid he frightened you."

" No," said Barbary. " Not more than I was already."

He spared her a kind, inquiring, unintelligent glance; he took then Father Roger's arm, and led him down the church to the window where the elder boughs waved, and the two cassocked clergymen clambered out into the sunlit wilderness.

"A type very droll," Raoul commented, with the detachment of his race.

Barbary sniffed, wiped her eyes, and picked up the kitten and her painting satchel.

"But he knew about hell," she returned. "You bring the radio. We'll sell some postcards now, then go down to the wharfs. Jock said his friend with a boat would take us out. . . . Jock told me yesterday about how he deserted."

"How did he desert?"

"It was when his battalion was ordered east, to fight the Japanese. He gave them the slip on his embarkation leave; he says a lot of them did. Jock said he didn't mind the Boches so much, but he was dreadfully frightened of the Japanese, because they torture their prisoners. Some men he knew had been taken, and escaped; they did frightful things to them, the worst tortures you can think of. So Jock decided he wouldn't go near them, and I think he was quite right."

"He was perfectly right," Raoul agreed. "I would not go near them myself. They are very dirty types, those yellow men. Civilised armies should not fight them; the risks are too great. However, the risks are formidable also with the Boches; they are often dirty types too."

Both looked, with oblique distaste, unto the dark pits of the past, from which anguished screams rose. Like Father Roger, they, too, knew about hell.

"Anyhow," said Barbary, quickly shutting the door on it, "that was why Jock deserted. And he's been on the

run ever since. So we must never tell anyone that we
know what he did. . . . He's got three ration books just
now, and all with his name on them. He says he didn't
steal them, he and Horace know a man who makes them."

"We should do well to have some more ourselves,"
Raoul suggested.

"The postcards are a shilling each," Barbary told two
ladies who stopped to look. They were standing in Fore
Street, outside the wall, outside the gate of Cripplegate, at
the door of the ruined café. Barbary's postcards were
spread out on the low wall.

"Look, Julia," the ladies told one another. "They are
really very nicely done. Did you paint them yourselves,
my dears?"

"Yes. I expect we are selling them too cheap. Would
you pay one and six?"

The ladies would. They were real ladies, and one and
six was chicken feed to them; they might have paid half
a crown if asked, for they liked bomb ruins, and liked to
take mementos of them back to Bournemouth, where they
lived.

Sometimes Americans would go by, and they liked bomb
ruins still more, not finding in Britain as many as they had
been led to expect, and wanting to convince their friends
back in Maine or Philadelphia that they had really seen the
scars of war. For the Americans Barbary put up the postcards to half a crown. When they went back to lunch
this Sunday, they had taken twenty-two and sixpence.

* 24 *

"A STRING bag's silly," said Mavis to Barbary. "Anyone can see what's in it, before you're out of the store. What you want is a good-sized canvas bag; not so big it looks funny, but big enough to hold what you slip in. Tins and things. Horace is for ever wanting canned anchovies; he can't get enough of them. I always have to get him some when I go shopping. After all, you can't let the boys go short, what with all they've been through and all the hiding about they have to do. Jock has a great liking for syrup and shell eggs, I expect he's told you. What's Raoul's special fancy?"

"Sardines, I think. And Camembert. But I shan't take anything for him, he has plenty to eat at home, so have I. I'll try and get Jock some syrup and shell eggs. . . . How often are you caught, Mavis?"

"Twice, I've been. I was once in the courts after going all round Selfridge's with my bag. You should have seen me—panties and stockings and lipsticks and a handbag and a lovely lighter for Horace—it broke my heart I didn't get away with it. I told them I'd been took giddy."

"Giddy?"

"Yes, that's what to say if you're nabbed. They all say it in the courts."

171

"But if I was giddy I should sit down, not put things in my bag."

"All the same, that's what to say. A friend of mine gets her lawyer to say it for her. Magistrates being mugs, they don't know how giddiness may take you. My friend says the beaks say to her, 'You are a perfectly respectable woman, and look how you steal.' She's ever so pleased, because it's the only time she ever gets called a perfectly respectable woman, you have to steal first."

Barbary thought that would be nice, to be called a respectable woman once in a way; for a maquisarde, that is something.

"Well," she said, "I'll try. My father will be very angry if I'm caught, though."

"He's a lawyer, isn't he? Why, he ought to come and defend you, and tell the beak how you came over giddy and hadn't ever done it before. I wish *my* dad was a lawyer. All *he* does is wallop me. I don't see him speaking up for me how I'd never stolen before."

"Mine wouldn't either. Because I've often stolen before."

"Why, bless you, so's everyone that does it now. They're all old hands. That's just beaks' nonsense, how people have always been respectable till they suddenly see something in a shop they fancy and fall for it. They'll say it of women who've done it all their lives. As if a woman who's lived up to thirty or forty without stealing is suddenly going to begin; she just wouldn't know how. One has to start early at that game. The trouble with beaks is they don't know human nature." Mavis, who prided herself

on doing so, knew at least that *nemo repente fuit turpissimus.*
Suddenly she sighed.

"But when I was nabbed, I couldn't help thinking to
myself, whatever would Mr. Monty have said? Because
Mr. Monty, you know, was a large-size, clever gentleman,
the things he did were all big, clever things. What I mean,
you can't fancy Mr. Monty snooping round a store with a
shopping-bag. He used to walk down the street there"—
she nodded in the direction of the grass-grown alley that
ran past the one-time premises of her late employers—
"swinging his little cane, his hat tipped sideways, and ever
so stout, not *too* stout, if you know what I mean, just
comfortable and handsome; us girls all had a crush on
Mr. Monty. I often think, as I stroll about here, what if I
was to see Mr. Monty stepping up Addle Street, his nosegay
in his button-hole and a matey word for all, what would
I do? Go right back to the old firm, I think, if it was
suddenly to build itself up again. Funny it would look, you
don't remember it, but just you fancy all these paths streets
again, and all these mucky pits full of great buildings, an'
all these stairs that run up to empty sky, Ladies and Gents
on every floor; just fancy, kid, if the offices and shops was
back on each floor, and business gentlemen sitting in them,
and the girls clacking away on the typewriters like street
drills, and the cups of tea being made and passed round
every two hours. Those were the days. Cripplegate an'
Aldermanbury and Wood Street an' Addle Street and
Basinghall and London Wall—oh, it was a nice neighbourhood then, most respectable, and yet full of life, see. A
business girl could step out of her office and there'd be

nice streets, jammed up with traffic and people, and there'd
be lots of shops and lunch places, and where you could get
cigs and chocs and have a cup o' tea. And look at it now,
I ask you, it gives me the creeps. All a mucky shambles,
nothing but these scrabbly bushes and nettles and cheap
weeds and caves and pits and smashed walls, an' all those
ruined churches. You didn't have to notice churches before;
there was too many, but they just stood back quiet and
tidy and said nothing—and now look at them, all bats and
ghosts I shouldn't wonder, an' all those windows and doors
hanging loose, they're awful. God's houses, I *don't* think.
Something ought to be done about it. Horace says it just
shows religion up, but I dunno. You religious, kid? "

" No. But I believe in hell."

" You do? Oh, well, who's to say you're wrong?
Must be something like that, you'd think, or where *are*
the wicked ones to go? "

" Oh, yes ; there is. So you have to repent before you
die. Of course there's no hurry, but you must make time
just before you die. It's awful if you're killed suddenly,
because then you're damned."

" Gracious, you know some language, don't you."

Barbary stared across ruins and brambles with melancholy
eyes. The girls were walking up towards Coachmakers'
Hall, after a mid-afternoon meal of coffee and cake in
Cheapside. It was the habit of Mavis and her friends to
have meals all day ; they barely paused between breakfast,
morning coffee, early lunch, afternoon coffee, afternoon
tea, late tea, supper, and bedtime snacks. All the tea-shops
were crowded with the continuous eating of such as Mavis

and her friends. Housewives out shopping paused in their labours to eat and to drink; in a sweet haze of coffee, of tea, and of pastries, their burdens lightened, slipped away, they forgot the rest of their shopping list and sat on, the white thick cups and plates clattering about them on marble tables, taken away, refilled, emptied again; so each meal slipped timelessly on into the next, until at last the eaters gathered up their shopping bags and went. It was the war that had done this to them, turning life into one continuous quest for food—food to take home, food to consume in shops, food no longer a means but life's great end. Rations, dictated by coupons, had to be bought; to leave them unbought would be a sinful waste; bacon, fats, sweets, biscuits, everything in tins, were week by week absorbed; people grew in stature and in weight, and clothes were let out.

So Mavis and Barbary, this August afternoon, walked up Noble Street to Coachmakers' Hall full of coffee and vile cakes.

" Another thing, kid. If you're going snooping in the stores, you must pay attention to how you look. What I mean—if you don't mind my saying it," Mavis politely interpolated, " you don't need to go about looking like a ragamuffin, in those sandshoes, and your hair flapping about all ways, and your hands dirty like they are now, and no paint on your nails, and not so much as a dab of lipstick. 'Tisn't human, if you don't mind my saying. And if you're going round the stores with a bag, looking like you do, people will keep their eye on you, watching to see you slip something. What's more, the beak won't believe you got a giddy turn, and he won't call you a respectable woman. No, really: you've got to doll up. I'll take you somewhere for a hair-do; you'd look good in curls, I'd say. And with your face done, and your mouth like other people's. Your eyes are ever so nice," Mavis added, generously. "What I mean, it'd do you good all round, besides in the stores, to have a smarten up. Jock'd like it. Don't you feel any pride in yourself? I never knew a girl go about as you do, and that's a fact. Funny your people let you, they living in a nice house like they do, and your Pa a swell lawyer or is he a judge? I should say they'd be pleased to see you walk in on them all smartened up, wouldn't they?"

"Shouldn't think they'd care. But if you think I'll get on better I'll do it."

"Good kid. I'll take you to my hair place to-morrow. Then you'll be all set for shopping."

They climbed down into the pit of Coachmakers' Hall. In the painted doorway of a cellar Horace sat reading.

"He's reading Aristotle," Mavis explained. "He's ever so fond of Aristotle. Hiya, Horace."

But Horace was not reading Aristotle; Aristotle lay on the ground beside him, disdainfully thrown down; Horace read the *Greyhound Express*. He looked up, sourly, and addressed Barbary.

"You brought me the wrong volume. It's called Ethics, and it's lousy. You'd better let me come in and pick one myself."

"All right. Coxy'll be out this afternoon till late, so we can all go in for a bit."

Barbary left them, to meet Raoul in Somerset Chambers.

"I am going shop-stealing to-morrow afternoon," she said, in French. "With the large bag. First it is necessary, Mavis says, that I have my hair curled and my face painted and my best clothes, as shop stealers have to be respectable. So I will have to have all that done to-morrow morning."

"Can I come shop-stealing too?"

"No. Boys get noticed in shops; it does not do. Except in tool shops and bicycle and radio shops. Jock says he picks up a lot of things in those. He slips them into his pockets. But in general shops it has to be women, with large bags and looking *comme il faut*. What shall I get for you?"

"I will have some Gruyère. If there is none, then Camenbert, well manured. That is from the food department. From others I will have a corkscrew-knife, a red scarf, and a flute."

Barbary wrote it down in her sketch-book.

"And I need a new bicycle bell," she said. "Please get one if you can."

* 25 *

BARBARY, with her hair cut in a neat rolled page-bob
to her shoulders, rouge on her cheeks, crimson lipstick
on her mouth, and scarlet polish on her nails, stirred Jock's
senses as she had never done before. Even Raoul liked to
walk close to her, holding her by the arm. Mrs. Cox said:
"Well, I never. So you've gone all fancy. And who may
that be for, I'd like to know? That Jock, I suppose."

"Oh, no. Jock doesn't matter. It's just to look respectable
in shops."

"Well." Mrs. Cox surveyed her, taking in the clean
primrose-yellow frock, the hair, the rouge. "Respectable,
you call it. If you ask me, it's getting near the other. But
girls will make dolls of themselves to-day, I know that.
You'll have to keep out of those nasty ruins, if you want
to keep nice. And what do you think you're going to buy,
taking that great bag?"

"It depends," Barbary told her, "what I see."

She saw much. Galaxies of desirable objects, glittering
into the focus of attainability, shone with a new moonish
lustre, as of fruit ripe for plucking and within reach. They
slid like dropping peaches into her bag, swept in by
annexing, furtive gestures. Wandering round laden counters

178

among crowds, she was carried away by the bounty of
opportunity and the ease of performance. She gazed like
Traherne,

> *Wondering with ravishment all things to see,*
> *Such real joys, so truly mine to be,*

and would have repeated, had she known the words,

> *Transcendant objects doth my God provide,*
> *In such convenient order all contriv'd.*

Returning laden from her tour, she stored her acquisitions
in a cavity in Barbers' Hall, screened from the entrance by
a thicket of bracken and chickweed. When she told Mavis
about them, Mavis said the thing was to sell most of them,
she knew of a place. Barbary said she would like to keep
some of the things, such as a musical-box, a yellow scarf
decorated with black kittens, a paint-box, a canary with a
whistle, a cushion with a handle, and a small alarm clock.
Raoul also would like to keep some things. Horace and
Jock, on the contrary, said Mavis, would, she knew, be for
selling everything, as they could use money. Barbary did
not tell Mavis where she had stored the things; the sly
secrecy of the maquis rose in her; she said she had hidden
them somewhere safe. She had, nevertheless, a notion that
Horace, informed by Mavis, might go searching in the
various caves and cellars of Cripplegate and Aldermanbury
which they all from time to time used. Or some other
vagrant, seeking shelter by night, might creep into Barbers'
Hall and burrow in among the bracken of Inigo Jones's
court-room, to find there not the ancient treasures, the gilt

cup with bells, the silver cup with gilt acorns dangling, the great silver bowl, the Holbein, the Van Dyck, the plaster fruit and flowers, but the big canvas shopping-bag squatting in a deep nest of marigolds and rose-bay willow herb, stretched plump with gaudy plunder. What a find! Barbary could not leave it unguarded, and did not dare to take it home: she told Mrs. Cox that she would be stopping the night with friends, collected Raoul, who would have to be home by ten, took supper, cushions and rugs, and encamped among the fern and boulders and wild garden of Inigo's hall.

It was a warm damp evening; a small wind wandered whispering about the long grass; smells of mould and earth, ruin, mortality and summer flowers, drifted here and there with acrid sweetness; from the salvage headquarters at the Aldermanbury-London Wall corner, where all night in a great cavern two men guarded treasures and tools, the smell of cooking over oil stoves stole down the moving air. Barbers' Hall was in Monkwell Street, lying against a great tree-grown bastion of the Wall, and under the shadow of St. Giles's; from it a narrow path ran into the churchyard. After supper, Raoul strolled about with a catapult, while Barbary painted postcards in the dying yellow light. Later there would be a nearly full moon; she meant to paint the bastion by moonlight; moonlight effects always sold well.

Raoul came into the cave with two shell eggs that he had found in a hen's nest in St. Olave's churchyard, but they had no means of cooking them. They played draughts for a while, for pennies, then Raoul read aloud *Les Mystères du Château Noir*, while Barbary painted.

" It would be nice," said Barbary, " to see a picture of all this as it was—all houses and offices and shops and streets. Mavis says it was much better then. But I don't know. I think I like it better like this. One belongs more."

" Perfectly," Raoul agreed. " This is more for us. It is *chez nous.*"

Then it was half-past nine, and he had to go. Neither thought or suggested that Barbary would feel lonely or nervous by herself all night in Barbers' Hall: children of the maquis, they were trained to lonely nights.

Raoul got his bicycle, that he had left chained to a stile, and rode home. Barbary strolled along Monkwell Street, Silver Street, London Wall, in the deepening dusk, picturing them as paved streets with great buildings, lights, doors, windows, shops, halls, where now ran dusky lanes, where now lay broken stones, where now the green world seeded and sprang. She knew nothing; she had never seen, nor would, that old pre-ruin world. She did not know how these city streets had appeared; how Fore Street had been dignified by Barclay's Bank at its Western end, jostling a merchant from Japan, close against St. Giles's church, and by the Westminster Bank beyond Cripplegate Buildings to the east. Somerset Chambers she knew, and the Zita Café; but Mr. F. C. Hart, maker of umbrellas, and Mr. Albert King, verger of St. Giles's, and Mr. Rand, who had made imitation jewellery, were not even phantoms in her mind. Neither could she know how the lane that had been Monkwell Street had run past the rich carved door of Barbers' Hall, and had been stately with ingenious men who had manufactured hats, mats, ties, underwear, account-books, typewriters, fancy goods, gloves and buttons, and busy with general merchants, those more versatile, less creative beings, traders living among makers. The little squares and courts between Monkwell Street and Wood Street were quite gone, as vanished as the twelve proper almshouses placed there by the mayor in 1575, wherein had lived twelve poor and aged persons on sevenpence a week and five sacks of charcoal a year for ever (but who has that charcoal now?). The twelve poor persons were avenged, for the great buildings that had replaced their almshouses were now one with them; the crickets in the brambly copse that sprawled where Windsor Court and Wood Street Square had been, chirped like the ghosts of a chatter of burned typewriters.

In Noble Street, past the Coopers' Arms, there had stood a hotel, the Post Office Hotel, kept by a Mrs. Blesser, and Peter Barbieri's refreshment rooms, and Stabney's Bar, and Gregg's Dining-rooms; in Noble Street one had never lacked for food and drink. Messrs. Parama, pausing in their manufacture of essential oil, Messrs. Henriques, weary of making velveteen, Mr. Rudolph Cohn, tired of gloves, could walk out and find elevenses and snacks all the street along, from Lilypot Lane to Falcon Square. In the narrow way of Addle Street, Lady Clare, Ltd., busily making corsets between Brewers' Hall and Philip Lane, could refresh herself at Lorenzo Cattivi's café down the street.

Poor merchants, poor manufacturers, poor agents, poor warehousemen, where are they all now? Blown sky high, burnt up by that horrid malicious bloody flame, many have seeded themselves again elsewhere, struggling valiantly against extinction. Others have vanished, destroyed utterly, and commerce knows them no more. In any case, they no longer flourish in Cripplegate, Aldermanbury and Basinghall; Monkwell and Addle Street ramble oblivious through stony deserts, and the pavements they so lately, so venally, trod are craters where the rose-bay and the chickweed sprawl. Their merchant integrity, such as it was, drifts dissolved and scattered on the seeding winds, their quaint honour turned to dust, and to ashes all their lust. Among the hidden Companies' Halls, deep below where guildmen had for centuries feasted and conferred, among the medieval bases and only a few feet now above the Roman stones, the lion and the lizard keep the courts where merchants gloried and drunk deep, the wild ass stamps, the wild cats scream, and the new traders, the pirates, the racketeers, the black marketers, the robber bands, roam and lurk. Commerce, begun in peddling and piracy, slinks down into peddling and piracy again, slinks guiltily among the shadows of the moon.

The moon was rising, apricot pink, blanching the dusky craters, the wild lanes, the broken walls. By its ivory light Barbary returned to Barbers' Hall, and, treading quiet and unseen at her heels, Horace suddenly appeared as she entered her recess. He followed her into the shadowed cave.

"What cheer, kid? How's tricks? Mavis said you did a grand job of work scrounging the shops. These the doings? Look, I've come to take them off you and sell them I know where. It's not safe, you being out here with them all night; bad characters might come along. There was a kid done in the other night, in some bombed building or other,

So you give them to your Uncle Horace to keep safe and sell for you."

"No," said Barbary, in a losing voice. "I want to keep some of them."

"Which?" He was turning them over in the bag. "The paint-box?"

"Yes. And the scarf and the musical-box and the whistling canary." She sat down on the leather cushion, concealing it, hugging her knees.

"Silly," said Horace. "You don't scrounge to keep, you scrounge for cash. I'll tell you what, you keep this bloody silly canary; it wouldn't fetch so much, and it's a kind of peculiar, fancy object, that the dicks look out for when they prowl round the fences. But keep it quiet, for Christ's sake; don't go whistling it about the streets. In fact, I believe I'd be a fool to leave it you, you've so little sense. Still, you scrounged it, Christ knows why, so you may's well keep it. You can't keep the scarf, you'd be wearing it, and those kittens catch the eye. . . . I'll take the things away in my case."

He shovelled them in. Barbary watched him, sulky and silent. He snapped the case shut, and smiled at her.

"There's a good chicken. Going home?"

"Not yet."

"Shall I stay with you for a bit?"

"No. I like it best alone."

"Be all right? What do you want to stay in this blinking hole for, with a nice bed at home? Expecting a friend? Jock, I wouldn't wonder."

"No."

She sat still, looking, Horace thought, rather fetching in
the moonlight, with her smooth page's bob and pink on
her cheeks. He had never admired her before, she was
not his style; now desire moved in him. He sat down at
her side and put his arm round her.

" Give us a kiss, chicken."

Sulky at having been outwitted and robbed, she pushed
him away and got up.

" No, why should I? You've stolen my things. I'm
going to my flat. You go home."

He did not really want her. A popular man, he had
better girls than this; nor would he risk offending Mavis.
He left her, slipping away through the shadowy halls and
lanes, skirting the shrub-grown walls of churches, on whose
vacant rubbled floors the spaces of the moon lay.

Into St. Giles's Barbary climbed through the west
window, to make her placatory devotions before the
phantom altar, lest death should come for her to-night and
hell yawn. Having made provision against this, she
attended to her temporal safety for the night by reciting lines
from the torn hymn-book pages that she kept in a niche in
the wall.

> *Bishop of the souls of men,*
> *When the foeman's step is nigh,*
> *When the wolf lays wait by night*
> *For the lambs continually,*
> *Watch, O Lord, about us keep,*
> *Guard us, Shepherd of the sheep.*
> *When the hireling flees away,*

Caring only for his gold,
And the gate unguarded stands
At the entrance to the fold,
Stand, O Lord, Thy flock before,
Thou the guardian, Thou the door.

It was too late, of course; the wolf had already forced his way into the unguarded gate of the fold and robbed the lambs; she should have remembered to pray it before. She climbed up to her flat in Somerset Chambers, where, curled up with rug and cushion, she fell asleep, her face hidden in her arm against the staring moon.

Waking, cramped and chilly, in the faint beginnings of dawn, she looked out from her terrace over the cold grey tumbled waste, the cratered landscape of the moon, and saw the great dome riding beyond it, pale curve of dove grey against a dove's breast sky. Mighty symbol dominating ruin; formidable, insoluble riddle; stronghold, refuge and menace, or mirage and gigantic hoax? Accepting it as the former, Barbary saluted it with a deprecatory sign of the cross, before picking up her belongings and descending the broken stairs to Fore Street.

Turning down Aldermanbury, she passed the great cavern where night watchmen kept guard over timber. There were two of them; elderly men making tea over an oil stove, an occupation they pursued all night. Barbary paused, looking in.

" Hallo," she said.

" Hallo, missie. Early, aren't you? Cup o' tea? "

" Yes, please."

She came in, and sat on a wooden seat. They gave her hot tea and bread and margarine.

" You're out early, my dear."

" I was out all night, actually. I'm on my way home now."

" All night, were you? You be careful, my dear. It's young girls like you get murdered. Murdered every night. And day. As often as not by their boy friends. There's great wickedness prowling about these days, great wickedness."

" Yes." They could tell her nothing about wickedness; she knew it all. She drank her tea and went down Aldermanbury and Milk Street to Cheapside and St. Paul's, and so home along Fleet Street and the Strand, which began to stir with early workers. She let herself into the house and crept silently upstairs; when six strokes chimed from all the false clocks, she was asleep in bed. Her last waking thought had been, to-morrow I shall get some more things, and this time I shall hide them here.

Mrs. Cox, hearing her come in, turned heavily over in bed. Staying with friends, indeed. Which of those young good-for-nothings does she go with? I ought to write to her Pa. *And* her Ma too. What's more, I will. Dear Sir, I will say, Dear Madam, I feel it my duty to speak my mind, for what goes on here you should know and what it will come to is beyond me to say, me that loved Miss Barbary when she was a mite and don't want her to come to harm, and young folks to-day unless watched and guarded very careful they do come to harm, the same as they always did but worse, now being frequently found in lonely places and bombed buildings in a state I don't need to remind you of, sir. Oh, madam, it may be far otherwise in France and those parts but here in England there is great wickedness and poor Miss Barbary the fact is she is keeping company she shouldn't do and many times I've told her but she pays no heed and when I hear her creeping in and out by night what she needs is a parent's care and well I remember how my husband used to take his belt to our Alice to keep her straight but straight was what our Alice never would grow to be. Oh, sir, oh, madam, I am saying what is my duty not what I would wish to say but I think you should know how it is. . . .

On a pleasant tide of helpful intention, flowing composition and bland treachery, Mrs. Cox drifted again into sleep.

* 26 *

I T was not to be expected; one could not get away with
it twice. Barbary, grown too confident, too little careful,
and companioned this time by Raoul, did the round of
St. Paul's churchyard, slipping unobtrusively from shop to
shop in the busy mid-afternoon. They left the churchyard
with a full bag, picked up their bicycles in Paternoster Row,
and rode them up Foster Lane to the stile across Noble
Street, where they chained and left them, Noble Street
being a footpath only. After investigating the clump of
fig-trees in St. Anne's and St. Agnes' churchyard, to see if
the tiny green figs were getting any riper, they crossed the
wilderness in the warm grey afternoon ; it smelt of wild
flowers and rain and dead rabbits. They did not go into
Barbers' Hall; that was where Horace would go, looking
for further caches of treasure. This time Barbary would,
after having some refreshment in Somerset Chambers, take
her loot home and hide it in her bedroom cupboard.

Past the Coopers' Arms, up the thread of Monkwell
Street, past Barbers' Hall, into the alley through St. Giles's
churchyard, round the church, past the Zita, which they
rejected as gaping too openly on the street, up the winding
stairs to their room, and in the room Horace sat on a roll

of matting and smoked. He said: "Halloalloallo. Thought you might be looking in. Going to have a snack, are you?"

Barbary fished in her bag, extracted two bottles of beer and some cake, and sat down cautiously on the bag.

"We're not staying long. We've got to get home."

"Well, what luck to-day? Show us."

"No luck."

"What d'you mean, no luck? That bag looks pretty fat to me."

Barbary and Raoul had their heads tilted back; warm beer, which they did not like, gurgled down their throats; they felt like two chickens drinking, watched by a fox. Raoul set down his bottle, wiped it, and ingratiatingly smiled at Horace.

"You will drink too?"

"Thanks, kid, I'll look in at Coopers' Arms for mine."

"Ha, ha," Raoul politely laughed at this well-worn jest.

Barbary thought, he means to get hold of it. If we can get to the bicycles, we shall beat him. She sat silent, thinking out a way to trick him.

Footsteps sounded, climbing the stone stairs; the doorway was darkened by two large dark blue forms, even as Horace sprang to his feet, standing alert and startled, the fox at bay.

So the Gestapo had tracked them down at last. Barbary sat still on her bag, staring up at them; Raoul stood beside her. Surprisingly, one of the Gestapo said, "Hallo, miss," and she saw that he was Henry, Mrs. Cox's nephew, whom she had met sometimes in the kitchen at home. Treachery,

treachery everywhere. Coxy was treacherous, a collabo; one could trust no one.

"Hallo, Henry," she replied sombrely.

"I must ask you," said the other gestapo, addressing Barbary and Raoul, "to come along with me to the station."

"What for?" But why ask? It would be for questioning, for torture, for beating up, for betrayal of secrets. They had followed from St. Paul's churchyard, tracking cautiously over the ruins; they knew about the bag.

"You were observed," said the gestapo, "appropriating articles in certain shops, and proceeding from the shops to this place. You had better come quietly, both of you youngsters."

He turned towards Horace, who stood smoking by the door.

"Nothing to do with me," said Horace. "I was sitting here having a bit of a rest, when these kids came up. I never saw them before, as a matter of fact."

"Have you your identity card?"

Horace rummaged in his pockets.

"No; don't seem to have it on me to-day. Funny, that is. I always carry it, as a rule. Funny your asking me for it just to-day. But that's how it goes."

"Well, I'll ask you to accompany us to the station too."

"What d'you mean? I've done nothing. I don't have to carry my bleeding card about wherever I go, just to please the bleeding coppers. You've nothing on me."

Sweat shone on his forehead. They had got him at last, and once they got you it was the end; everything came out.

The years stretched in front of him, dizzily dark; better anything than that. Quick as a cat, he leaped for the door before they could seize him, and raced down the stairs. They followed on his heels; one of them dashed after him into Fore Street, blowing his whistle; the other, Mrs. Cox's Henry, stopped at the foot of the stairs, ran up them again to the top flat. He was too late; he picked up the bag, but his prey had escaped on to the terrace; through the great stone jamb which had held the east window they looked down on the naked church floor below. The policeman appeared on the terrace. Barbary swung herself through the window, dropped lightly on her feet, raced up the church to the sacristy at the west end, where the great green bronze bells lay wrecked, with John Milton, upright and austere, looking gravely down on them.

Raoul, climbing through the window after her, was clutched by the shoulder, hauled back, dragged down the stairs, out into Fore Street, and into St. Giles's by the door.

"Where's she gone?" the policeman asked. "Is she hiding in the church?"

"I know nothing." Raoul repeated the maquis formula.

Henry marched him up the church, and glanced into the sacristy.

"Got away through there, I suppose," he concluded, looking at the window with the elder tree outside it.

They tramped out of the church, and began to scour the maquis, climbing down into pits and cellars, searching the caves of the companies' halls, beating about among deep brambles and tall weeds, flushing rabbits and rats.

The other policeman was out of sight, pursuing Horace

through the alleys and thickets of Cripplegate and Aldermanbury. The ghosts of Noble Street and Addle Street
crowded to their vanished windows to watch the chase;
the landlady of the Post Office Hotel at the corner of
Lilypot Lane, the drinkers in the Coopers' Arms and in
Peter Barbieri's refreshment rooms, the makers of gloves, of
ties, of velveteen, of ladies' underwear and of essential oil,
the warehousemen of Addle Street and Gresham Street.
Lady Clare, Ltd., glanced disdainfully down from her
corset manufactory, Lorenzo Cattivi stared with Italian eyes
from his café, Rudolph Kohn with Hebrew ones from his
gloves, the vicars, vergers and congregations of St. Alban's,
St. Mary's Aldermanbury, St. Anne's and St. Agnes', St.
Laurence Jewry's, and St. Vedast's who had been St. Foster,
the companies' guildmen in their halls, the Jews in a score
of business blocks, all gazed respectably down at the fleeing
criminal, the pursuing police, lending the law the silent
support of some eight centuries of property and substance.

But Horace had the heels of them all, and got away,
losing himself in a warren he knew, from which a tunnel
ran down to Cheapside and the liberty of crowds.

The ghosts drew back, went on manufacturing, trading,
warehousing, conferring, drinking, praying, vergering,
telling their money, among the empty shadows of the grey
afternoon, whispering together among the nettles, the fireweed, the nightshade, the bryony and the timothy grass,
sighing that all was over with the world and the British
Way of Life if criminals could get so easily away. The
policeman, better adjusted to post-war standards and the
British Way of Life, shrugged his shoulders and turned back

to assist his colleague in flushing Barbary, so mysteriously gone to earth; she might have been Daphne transformed not into laurel but into the elder tree that rustled at St. Giles's window, creaking and scraping at the iron frame.

Inside the bronze bell lying on its side in the sacristy, Barbary lay curled, hearing the Gestapo crashing about the maquis outside. Her first impulse was to lie hid until the hunt was over. Then she thought of Raoul, fallen into Gestapo hands, being dragged off to the cells for questioning. That would not do; she must somehow get Raoul free. Warily she crawled out of the bell and into the church; from the window she watched Henry, gripping Raoul firmly by the arm, climbing in and out of the caves of Barbers' Hall, parting the jungle weeds and brambles to peer among them. It struck her that if she broke from hiding into the open it would startle Henry, he might let Raoul go and pursue her; then they could both, with their intimate knowledge of the ground, surely outwit and evade him.

She climbed through the window, dropped into long grass, and started to run across the waste. Henry turned and saw her;] shouting, he gave chase; with Raoul in tow, he had not a chance. His quarry skipped like a hare from wall to broken wall, leaping chasms and darting up and down cliffs; she had crossed Wood Street and reached Addle Street and Philip Lane, and was running between St. Alban's and St. Mary the Virgin's, when the other Gestapo appeared, having renounced Horace, walking up Wood Street towards St. Alban's. Barbary saw him suddenly, as she ran along a broken edge of wall; startled, she forgot to look where she trod, stepped forward into nothingness, plunged steeply down a chasm into the stony ruins of a deep cellar, and there lay still beneath a thorn-apple bush, among the medieval foundations of Messrs. Foster, Crockett and Porter's warehouse. They—Messrs. Foster, Crockett and Porter—had been used to make surgical instruments, which were what she would now require.

* 27 *

HELEN had a bad attack of gaming fever, which had to be worked out; it was like a drunkard's thirst, which must be quenched. So, while Lucien took his wife and children to Ste. Maxime for the bathing (he doted on his children), Helen took Richie and Roland to Monte Carlo for the gambling. They lost more than they won; the losses were Helen's, the gains Richie's, who had beginner's luck; Roland, who would have had still more of this, did not yet play, except with his mother on the sands. Helen before long had lost all she had brought; she borrowed from Richie, and lost that; she sold a diamond ring to Mr. Max Intrator, and lost that too; she sent a cheque to her bank at Perpignan, but Perpignan banks in August are somnolent and in no hurry to answer; indeed, they are only open for so brief a time each day that they can scarcely hope, and indeed do not hope, to perform their business.

Anyhow, Helen and Richie and Roland stayed on in their Monte Carlo hotel, resigned to their plight, unable to gamble or to pay their bills, but enjoying themselves in their quiet way.

" People used to play for their horses and their estates and their mistresses," Helen said, as they sat on the balcony after dinner. "I could stake the car, I suppose, and the Fraises, and Lucien, and you and Roly. Only the croupier wouldn't particularly want any of them except the car, and I can't spare that. Never mind; I quite like Monte, though of course it's too full of people one knows. We might go into Italy to get more warmth and peace. But on the whole I think we'll stay where we are. Do you want to dine with the Chichesters at Cap Martin on Sunday? I don't, but you go if you feel like it."

"Yes, well, I do rather. Their dinners in London are entertaining."

"I dare say. Are they? I forget. Molly Chichester is a bright bore, more or less; but Brian is company. I'll accept for you, then, darling. . . . It reminds me of London dinners, when I would accept for Gully and refuse for myself. Hostesses don't mind if it's that way round; they can always get women."

"What I seem to remember," Richie said, "is your going out sometimes when people came to dinner at home."

Helen sighed. "Yes, my dear. I am afraid I did; and it was too bad. I wish my manners were better. Your father and you would never have done that. I suppose I have a phobia about being bored, and I indulged it."

"Why did you and Daddy invite bores?"

"The bores had invited us, no doubt. I dare say to some of the dinners I cut. Not that most of them were bores, exactly. A lot were legal, and legal men aren't often bores. But their wives sometimes are."

"What were they like?"

"Stupid, perhaps . . . isn't it that, as a rule? Or, anyhow,

not intelligent enough. Some of them wouldn't go through
a door, even though they were nearest it, but would hang
back and wait for the other women to go before them,
and there'd be a kind of polite, ridiculous wrangle. I
expect they thought me rude and arrogant for not doing
the same ... Don't you go and marry a stupid woman,
my dear. I should be a bad mother-in-law to her. What
would matter much more, you would probably end by
being a bad husband."

"Should I? But I think women *are* mostly rather stupid,
aren't they? Not nearly all, of course. Should one mind?
It's so much better than being pompous."

"Oh, much. Why, though, be either? You know, I
have always had women friends. They have never bored
me; I chose them too well. You can find them anywhere
if you look. I like them clever, curious about life, able and
apt to speculate and discuss, not too solemn, funny, knowing
about something, or a little about things in general, sceptical,
witty, bawdy if they like, first-hand, free; cultured or
philistine as they choose, so long as it's first-hand. I've
known plenty; some in Paris, some in London, some in
the universities, even some in Ireland, some married, some
single, some libertines, some unconcerned with all that.
Yes; one can always find them. So it's no use just saying
'women are stupid' and sitting down under it. Unfortunately few of your father's friends had wives of that
kind. Indeed, they weren't usually of that kind themselves.
So I wasn't always in to my own dinner parties. Well, it
was wrong; but it can't be helped now."

Richie did not care to say how wrong he held it to have

been; how mannerless, how unfair to his father, how lacking in all civility. Behind his impassive face and ironic brows disapproval coolly dwelt; he ranged himself with his father, with the conventions, with law and order, with the lawyers and their wives sitting down, embarrassed, to a dinner without a hostess. He felt that he and his fellows could not have struggled through so frightful, so hideously uncongenial a war, only to be rewarded with barbarism, with one's mother going out for her own dinner parties, besides running away with Frenchmen and leaving her family in the lurch. Further, he did not think that he would care to marry the kind of women from whom his mother chose her friends; they might be amusing intellectual company, but for himself, for a wife, he would prefer something more graceful, adaptable, conventional, lady-like, less, perhaps, pronounced, more suited, as it were, to the Corps Diplomatique. A gentle, merry slip of a girl, he pictured her, exquisite bud of some ancient tree, the prettiest deb of her year, never bawdy, perhaps a little High Church. Not one of those mocking, free-spoken Bohemian intellectuals of Bloomsbury, Newnham, or the Quartier Latin. If she should bore his mother, better so than that she should jar on him. As to his father, she would be the right, desired daughter; as to his sister, they need not meet much.

When he hinted something of this, Helen said, quizzically agreeing, that she thought he was entirely right.

" And I'm so glad," she added, " that you are going in for such an intelligent, *industrious* profession. So many young men want to take up writing. Of course it must be

199

charming to sit and write, and be supported by one's parents or someone else while one writes; I remember how charming I found it to sit and paint in Paris, on an allowance from my father in Ireland. But in the end one only adds to the mass of mediocre writing and mediocre painting that litters the world."

" Mediocre? Your painting? That's not what it's ever been called. . . ."

" Oh, I might, I suppose, have been some good if I'd worked. But one doesn't work; no amateurs do. Not with the seducing world all round them, enticing them, wasting their time and energies. Such pleasures! Wine, men and song. And dicing and gaming, and seeing the world. No, one doesn't work. Much better be a diplomat, a charming young First Secretary or attaché, all tidy and elegant and full of languages, with C.D. on your car and a tank full of petrol, discussing with your friends whether you'd like Paris, Washington, Rome or Teheran. That's seeing the world in style, and the pleasures offer themselves by the way, and you're paid for it. I shall be proud of you, Richie. You'll be so unlike me. At least I shall have produced *one* civilised child."

She had a little sigh for the other, and said, to put her out of mind, " Shall we play chess? "

As they rose to go in, a page came out with a telegram. Helen opened it; it had been sent on from Collioure. It said: "Barbary seriously injured bad fall some danger Deniston." It was dated two days ago.

She stood still, immobilised by shock. One hand went up to her forehead, as if to steady and arrange her thoughts.

" Can we get places on the Nice-London plane in the morning? Please telephone at once. . . . Some danger . . . *How much danger?* It took two days coming. By now, what has happened? What did they do to her . . . how did she fall? In the street? Oh, why no more than this, why not tell me more. . . ."

* *28* *

Monte Carlo came through just before midnight. Sir Gulliver was with the doctor in Barbary's room, and Pamela took the call.

"Sir Gulliver Deniston? ... Oh ... I see. ... I am Helen Michel. How is Barbary? ... No change? ... How much danger is there? Please tell me."

"There is some. The doctor doesn't know. He is with her now. She is still unconscious. . . . Yes, concussion. And her back—not broken, but wrenched. And, of course, shock. We can tell you more to-morrow. . . . It was in the ruins near St. Paul's—running from the police."

"I shall be in London to-morrow. I am flying from Nice in the morning. My sons too. We shall be with you to-morrow evening."

"Your sons? ..."

But Monte Carlo had faded out. Pamela sat with the receiver in her hand. Then Sir Gulliver came down with the doctor, talking in low, restrained danger-voices in the hall. Pamela heard the front door shut; Sir Gulliver came in to her, grave and tired.

"Nothing new," he said. "Anything may happen. She may become conscious before morning, or to-morrow, or not at all. If she does, the nurse will call me at once. You had better go to bed, dear."

"There's been a call, Gully. From France. She's flying to-morrow; here in the evening."

"With Richie, of course?"

"Yes. . . . She said, with her *sons* . . . at least I thought so."

"Her sons? Nonsense, you must have misheard. She would hardly bring a baby on such a journey, at such a time. Son, she must have said."

"I suppose so. Where will she stay? The Savoy is the nearest."

"She must decide that herself. She may want to be in the house, to be at hand all the time."

"In the house? But that's impossible."

"No, there's room."

"Room, yes. But still it's impossible. You know it is. The position . . . so impossibly odd."

"Odd, no doubt. But not impossible. Oddity must take a back place when life is in danger. Of course she must be in the house with Barbary if she wants to be."

"If they'd taken Barbary to a hospital, she couldn't have been."

"But as she's here, she can be. I agree that it's awkward, and will make a difficult situation for us all. *She* won't even notice it; she takes such matters in her stride. And, anyhow, her mind will be entirely occupied with Barbary."

"You'll hate it, Gully."

To so obvious a truth, he made no answer.

"And I shall hate it. And Richie'll hate it. And the

203

servants will think it most extraordinary. Gully, I do honestly feel she'd better sleep at a hotel, and come and visit Barbary from there."

" She can do so if she chooses. If she wishes to sleep here, she can do that too. She may want to be at hand through the nights. In fact, I fully expect that she will want to. She has always loved Barbary more than anyone else. When the child nearly died of meningitis, she slept in her room."

" Well, she seems, surely, to have rather pushed her off now."

Pamela, tired and overwrought, spoke crossly. He looked at her with some vexation.

" You don't know what you're talking about. You had better go to bed, hadn't you. I shall sit up for a time, in case I am wanted. I have letters to write."

Pamela went upstairs. She knew that she must keep calm and take care of herself and not worry. Apprehension filled her mind and stretched her nerves. She felt aggrieved at the extraordinary turn things had taken. It really was the limit. Barbary stealing from shops, chased by policemen, having that frightful fall, being taken not to a hospital but, owing to that stupid nephew of Mrs. Cox's, to Adelphi Terrace, Gully and she wired for, arriving to find the poor girl lying between life and death, the whole house having to be upset with day and night nurses, and nothing ready; Gully worried to death, all the good of Arshaig undone for him, herself feeling sick and despondent, Mrs. Cox and the servants gossiping together and with everyone who came to the house, about the dreadful business of Miss

Barbary and the shops and the bad company she had been
mixed up with, and some of it had got into the papers too.
And now Helen descending upon them, to create this quite
impossible situation. Would she have the common sense,
the ordinary good feeling, to realise that the situation would
be, quite literally, impossible? That she must not, in fact,
create it, but must sleep and eat in a hotel? Having no
reason to believe that Helen had either common sense or
ordinary good feeling, Pamela took a poor view of the
prospect ahead. She felt certain that the proprieties would
be outraged, Gully made acutely miserable (already he was
wretched enough about his unlucky, disreputable, possibly
dying daughter) and embarrassed beyond bearing, Mrs. Cox
and the char and the day and night nurses and the women
who obliged all delighted with the whole affair. As, indeed,
all their friends must necessarily be. Helen's old friends,
Helen's old enemies, Gully's acquaintances (lawyers were
such gossips), her own friends. She could go and stay with
her parents, of course, to evade the awkwardness of daily
intercourse between present and past wife; but that would
only make more and worse talk. No, she must face it,
carry it, while it lasted, calmly off. She would be, after all,
in the stronger position, doing what everyone would allow
was the fine and generous thing. Bohemians, Pamela
reflected, would think nothing of it; they were for ever
mixing up past and present consorts, with no embarrassment
in the world, even with apparent nonchalance, zest, and
good fellowship and the suggestion of a joke. But she was
no Bohemian; she had been brought up far from that
dubious and indelicate sea coast. And now Bohemia was

sweeping tempestuously into her home, and certainly with no notion of the difficulties of post-war English life, or even of the necessity of emergency food coupons; not, of course, that those could not be arranged easily enough. If the rest were as simple as that. . . .

Pamela went despondently to bed. Her last conscious thought was, I won't have Gully hurt: deep beneath it shivered the less conscious, I won't have Gully charmed. Her apprehensive, practical, experienced mind knew darkly that Gully might well be both.

She woke later saying, sharply, "People ought to be taken to hospitals, not to houses."

Gulliver was moving about the room; he looked at her, went back into his dressing-room, and shut the door.

* 29 *

THEY arrived at tea time. Hearing them at the door, Sir Gulliver came out of the library to meet them. Mrs. Cox hurried from the kitchen to help. Helen stood in the open doorway, while Richie brought in suitcases and paid the taxi. Tall and full-figured, golden-skinned, a red scarf turbaning her dark head, she held by the hand a plump dark-eyed child in a blue smock. Her eyes searched Gulliver's face for news.

" Tell me quickly, please. How is she ? "

" Very little change. She opened her eyes this morning, and was very sick; the doctor thinks that a good sign. She is unconscious now, but may come to at intervals. She has a good chance."

" I must go to her at once."

" I think you had better wait a little and rest. Will you have some tea ? "

" No, no. There was tea on the plane."

She looked past him, and saw Mrs. Cox.

" Coxy—how nice to see you."

" Oh, ma'am, oh, ma'am." Mrs. Cox came forward; tears ran down her broad pale cheeks; she clasped Helen's hand in both hers. " And the dear little fellow, too. . . ."

" Oh, yes; I forgot. Gully, this is Roland, my little boy. I had to bring him; there was nothing else, at the moment, to do with him. Besides, Barbary dotes on him, and I thought seeing him would help her to get better. So we brought him with us. Coxy will look after him, won't you, Coxy? And he can play with yours."

" As it happens, David is in the Isle of Wight."

" Oh. Then Roly can play by himself; he's quite used to that. . . . I can stay here, Gully? You can put me up? I must, you see, be on the spot."

" Yes," he agreed. " We expected that you would stay here. Mrs. Cox will show you your room."

" And Roly can sleep with me."

Gulliver looked down at the child, who looked up at him with merry dark eyes. Richie came in, pale and languid, still feeling airsick.

" Dear papa," he murmured. " We had the bumpiest passage. What about tea? "

" Poor Richie," his mother said. " He felt ill on the plane. Roly and I didn't. Go and get some tea, dear. Coxy, please take Roly and me upstairs. He must have a rest. And I want to go to Barbary."

They went upstairs, Roly holding a hand of each. They put him to lie down on David's cot; Mrs. Cox, delighted with him, begged that he might sleep in her room. Having disposed of him, they went to the room where Helen was to sleep. Here, while Helen washed her hands and face, Mrs. Cox told her the story of the disaster, luxuriating in the tragic tale.

" Oh, dear madam, the company the poor lamb got

208

into, and she so innocent, she didn't guess. I warned her,
I did my best to warn her, but she wouldn't heed. Oh, I
knew things were as they shouldn't be, and I planned
writing to Sir Gulliver in Scotland, but before I could
write . . . You see, ma'am, the poor lamb had run away
from Scotland and come home, and her father followed
her and gave her a talking, and left her with me to mind.
But what could I do? Oh, I knew things weren't right,
the *young men* she would bring to the house, but I didn't
let them through the door, I knew they was up to no
good, and I told her so. It's my belief, ma'am, they was
spivs, and army deserters too. Not that I ever thought she'd
let them *make free*, oh, no, I didn't think the poor lamb
would forget herself so far, but young men do take
advantage, as well we know. And besides that, what
mischief they might be leading her into, her and that little
French boy she was always with (your stepson, ma'am, to
be sure, I forgot)—well, who could answer that? So I
spoke to my nephew Henry, he's in the Force, and his
beat is round here, and one evening he looked in with a
friend, and I told them they must have her followed next
day and see where she went and what she was up to, so they
followed her to St. Paul's Churchyard, and it was just
what I suspected after I'd seen the things she brought in,
she went round the Churchyard shops with the French boy,
slipping things into a bag like those wicked women who
make a practice of it. Then off the two bicycled to them
nasty ruins where Miss Barbary likes to sit and paint all
day, and they fell in with one of those bad young men at
the top of a blitzed building, and Henry and his friend

surprised them and they all ran, and the young man got
clean away, they have so much experience, those young
men, no one can ever catch up with them, it's the war
taught them to run and hide and protect themselves with
wiles like creatures of the wild. But the French boy was
caught, and poor Miss Barbary fell to her death. Oh,
ma'am, how I blame myself, but indeed I acted for the
best, thinking the police had better keep an eye on her and
her friends that were no friends to her, knowing as how Sir
Gulliver wished for no more trouble, poor gentleman.
And now there the poor lamb lies between life and death
and nurses night and day. Her ladyship was vexed that
they didn't take her to hospital instead. But, oh, dear
ma'am, I know you'd choose for her to be under your
eye."

Helen heard the story, as she washed, combed her hair,
changed her shoes. How like, she thought, London was to
Collioure, the maquis of the city to the maquis of the Forêt
de Sorède. How much at home Barbary must have felt,
hiding and being chased about the ruins with Raoul and
spivs and deserters. Caelum non animum mutant qui trans
mare currunt: the maquis is within us, we take our wilderness
where we go.

Under her eye? Yes, indeed, she would choose Barbary
to be that, for ever that. Never again, if she lived, should
Barbary be taken from her. She could run wild in France
as well as in London, and with more love. *My* little girl, no
one else's. I shall take her back with me . . . if she lives.
She has no business here. Why did I send her? Because of
Maurice only; because of Maurice. And now there's

Lucien, and they shall be friends, and if she won't be, it's Lucien who must go, not my child, not Barby. She's always been first; she always will be, whatever she does. Now I must go to her, I must see her.

"Thank you, Coxy. Nothing has been your fault; she lived like that in France too. It's the war, and all they got caught up in through it. I shall go to her now."

"Oh, dear madam, it's like old times to see you home, and arriving with that bonny boy too. Nothing has been the same since you left."

"Better, I expect. Meals more regular, and all that."

She did not stay to hear tales of her successor; she crossed the passage to the darkened room in which Barbary lay bandaged and still, heavily breathing, while the day nurse sat in an arm-chair by the bed, reading *No Orchids for Miss Blandish*. She looked up at the large handsome woman who came softly in; this must be the patient's mother from France, of whom Mrs. Cox had told her. Mrs. Cox had been right about her beauty. Lady Deniston was a good looker, but her predecessor was something more. Even straight from the plane she came in looking like a film queen.

Nurse Ryan got up. She was fair, freckled and Irish.

"May I take your place, nurse, for a time? I'll call you if anything is needed."

"Well, I'm not sure I ought to leave the room. . . . Suppose she was to waken and want something in a hurry. The basin, it might be."

"Oh, I'll manage that. And I'll call you. Go and have a rest and a cup of tea." Helen remembered the formula

—how one must always mention the cup as well as the tea, how the thought of the china receptacle seemed to add comfort to the British soul.

" I've had my tea, thank you. But it could be no harm if I slip away for a bit."

" Does she breathe so heavily all the time? "

" All the time from the first. It's the way they have in concussion."

" Yes. What do you expect, nurse? "

The direct glance of those startling tawny eyes trapped Nurse Ryan into the truth, which it was against her professional principles to tell the relations.

" It could go either way. Still, while there's life there's hope."

" I see."

Helen sat down by the bed; Nurse Ryan slipped out, a slave to sudden passion. She met Mrs. Cox outside the door.

" She told me to go, while she sits there a while. You have to do what she says, she's so commanding. What did you tell me her name is now? "

" Madame Michel. She's widow to a poor French gentleman that got drowned last year. She's brought her little boy over, the sweetest duck. It's a funny position, nurse, I expect you're thinking."

Mrs. Cox led the way into the room where Roland lay on David's cot. There, in whispers, they discussed the funny position exhaustively.

Downstairs, Richie and his father were having tea together. They talked of Barbary.

"I shouldn't," Sir Gulliver said, "have left her alone here. I ought to have foreseen that she would get into a scrape. It seems that she kept very undesirable company. And hung about those Cripplegate ruins all day. Why, I don't know. She had no interest in archaeology, or medieval or Roman discoveries. Of course she painted there. . . ."

"It was more that she felt, I think, at home there. And liked playing at houses; and playing at the maquis. And, quite simply, liked ruins. As to the rest of it—the stealing from shops—that was no doubt suggested to her by her friends."

"She did steal." Sir Gulliver had brought himself, in these last days, to face the truth about his daughter. "She took some money from Arshaig when she left it. She promised me not to steal again. I see I was wrong; I ought to have known it would be too difficult for her, left alone in London, and mixing with such companions. I blame myself very much. If she recovers, I shall try to get her under better influences."

"I think mother wants to take her back to France, and let her learn painting in Paris."

Sir Gulliver, with raised brows, coldly rejected this scheme.

"Impossible. The worst thing for her."

For look, his silence seemed to say, at the result of seven years in France with her mother.

At this point Pamela came in, handsome and trim in a dark silk suit.

"Oh, hallo, Richie, how are you? I hear Madame

Michel is upstairs with Barbary. I hope you had a good passage."

"No, they're so bad, aren't they. Dreadful vehicles. I still feel ill."

"Oh, you're a namby. God, the tea's cold. No, it won't run to another pot. The ration never lasts out as it is; I think they drink it all up in the kitchen. I hope Madame Michel will get her emergency coupons to-morrow."

"She doesn't drink much tea."

"Well, tea's not all, is it? There are all the other things. I don't suppose she has much idea yet of how we live here."

"We live here much better than people do in France, actually."

"Oh well, in France there's always the black market. No one with money need go short. Here it's fair shares for all, but not much of them. Milk's the worst headache, while David's away."

"There'll be Roly's milk."

"Whose?"

"Roly's. Roland Michel, my infant stepbrother."

"Your . . .? Gully, what does he mean?"

"What he says. Helen has brought her son with her."

Pamela's clear brown skin slowly turned red; her black brows drew together.

"Gully, she *can't* have."

This valueless contribution to the conversation dissolved in the silence that engulfed it. Then Richie explained, tentatively, "Roly was with us at Monte Carlo. There wasn't much else to do with him. It seemed the simplest plan to bring him along."

" *Simplest* . . ." Pamela's annoyance was so great that she could not find the fitting words for it.

" And who's going to look after him? His mother will be with Barbary—at least, that's the reason she gave for coming."

" No doubt," said Sir Gulliver, " Mrs. Cox will be delighted to take care of him. And when David comes back his nurse can look after both children."

" David won't come back till Madame Michel is gone. It would be very inconvenient. And her child would bully David; he's two years older, isn't he? "

" A year and a half," Richie murmured. " But kindly disposed. I don't know that he is much of a bully, except to his nurse."

" Oh, he has a nurse. I wonder she wasn't brought too. A few more or less, what difference does it make? "

Sir Gulliver got up and left the room.

" I should think he's pretty sick about it all," Pamela said. " This child is more than he bargained for."

" Well, no one actually bargained at all, did they? We just wired and came. I'm sorry if it's very inconvenient. Shall I go away somewhere? "

" Heavens, no. You're the one bright spot. Imagine what dinner table conversation will be like—Gully all stiff and difficult, making conversation, me feeling awkward, your mother——"

" *Not* feeling awkward, I assure you. She takes it all quite naturally. In fact, she is only thinking about Barbary. She's desperately anxious, you know."

Pamela said nothing. She drank her cool tea and ate a piece of cake.

" My dear Richie," she said then, " of course we shall all do our best to make things go off not too badly, but you do realise, don't you, that it's going to be hell ? "

" Well, need it be ? Divorced people do meet, you know, and are often quite friendly and placid."

" They don't usually stay in the house with the next wife. *And* bring their children by the man they went off with. Do you realise this may last for weeks ? Barbary won't be able to be moved for ages, even if——"

" Even if she lives. If she dies, that will shorten my mother's visit, of course."

" It seems to me a pity to talk like that, as if you didn't care twopence whether she lives or dies. Of course she did behave awfully, and it's all a frightful disgrace; but, after all, she *is* your sister."

" True."

" Well, I must go and see to things. What have they done with the child ? "

" I've no idea. Something suitable to his years, no doubt."

Pamela guessed as much; she went straight to the nursery, and, as she had expected, perceived the foreign infant reposing on David's cot in his underwear. She looked down on the chubby brown face and tightly shut eyes and slightly open rosy mouth. Less handsome than his mother, she noted with satisfaction; probably like his father. Much bigger than David: whatever Richie said, he *would* bully David if they met. Meanwhile he would probably steal the affections of the fickle Mrs. Cox, who now came into the room, smiling fatuously on the cot.

"Well, my lady, isn't he a little duck? And big! Why he's twice David's size."

"He's twice David's age. Is he to sleep in the cot?"

"Well, seeing it's empty, it would seem only natural. Unless madam had him in with her, but the bed's not very large, it would be disturbing. I thought I'd move the cot into my room. Of course when our little man comes home, that'll be different."

"I shan't have David home at present; the house is much too full, and with illness too, and the nurses, there simply wouldn't be room. If the Shanklin lodgings can't keep them on, I must get him in somewhere else."

"And that's only natural," Mrs. Cox said, and nodded twice as she tucked in the blanket. "Not but that it would be pretty to see them running about together, the sweet ducks."

There was commotion on the stairs, and the thump of feet. Into the room came David and his nurse Alice.

Pamela caught him up in her arms.

"Oh, my sweetie. . . . But, Alice, why? What's happened? You weren't to come back till next week—and I was going to write to you to stay on longer."

"Oh, my lady, didn't you get my wire? There were measles in the lodgings—at least it was spots, and the doctor wasn't sure, so I thought I should bring baby away at once. I think he's all right, I don't think he's been in touch, but I dursen't risk staying on."

"No, of course. You were quite right, Alice. But the

217

house is rather full, you see, with visitors and nurses, and Miss Barbary ill, so I must send him away somewhere else. Look, there's even another little boy in his cot."

The other little boy opened dark slits of eyes and sat up, smiling at them. Hospitable and expansive, he made them welcome to his bedchamber. He exchanged penetrating stares with his contemporary; then David, with squeaks of indignation, began to pummel him with his fists. He pummelled back; slithering out of the cot in his vest and pants, he charged David like a bull calf, shouting war-cries, and pushed him down on the floor. David yelled; his mother picked him up and soothed him.

" I told you," she said to Mrs. Cox, " that he would bully David. We mustn't leave them alone together."

Upon the scene of tumult entered Helen, drawn by her son's shouts.

" Darling, you must be quiet," she was beginning; then perceived the multitude—Pamela, Mrs. Cox, Alice, the two belligerent infants. It was not the happiest introduction to Pamela; but none would have been happy. She turned to her with outstretched hand.

" Pamela, isn't it ? . . . We met once or twice, years ago— you can only have been about twenty. It's good of you to endure this invasion. I owe you so much apology—but I find it difficult to think about anything but Barbary at present. And now my son and yours have got together; I hope they will get on."

" How do you do. Our baby and his nurse have came home unexpectedly from the Isle of Wight. I must send him away again; there isn't room for him."

218

" Oh, surely. Roly will sleep with me; David will have his own cot of course. What a pretty child. He is like you."

Pamela did not say whom she supposed Roly to be like.

" If my parents can have him," she said, " I shall send him there. Two children together would make quite too much noise for Barbary. It would be better for her if we could get her to a hospital."

Helen shook her head, decisively.

" She can't be moved. And I must be in the house with her. I do apologise, I really do; I know it's frightful for you. But she may become conscious at any time, and I must be there. . . . Coxy, do you think you could keep Roly quiet, give him some supper, and then put him to bed in my bed ? "

Who *pays* Mrs. Cox, I should like to know ? flashed through Pamela's mind.

" We dine at eight," she said, " if that will be all right for you. I'm afraid our meals are rather austere—not, I expect, what you're used to in France. Our meat ration is so tiny."

Helen looked at her vaguely, as if she were failing to focus on the tiny meat ration.

" I must go back to Barbary. The nurse thinks she is breathing more naturally; she may come to."

She left behind her a curious, stirred, charged atmosphere. Pamela went to her room, holding her son by the hand.

30

Dinner was less difficult than might have been expected.
They all talked; tacitly agreeing that Barbary's plight
had better be a skeleton at the feast than one of the dishes
to be discussed, and all four being practised in worldly ease,
there were no awkward silences; they spoke of France, of
Britain, of the new government, of food difficulties, of the
black market at home and abroad, of friends. Helen asked
about acquaintances; Gulliver told her stories of them;
it was one of the occasions when he chose to be amusing
company. We are passing it off well, thought Richie, with
a sigh of relief. His mother, sitting opposite him, shone in
ivory beauty, in an old woollen dress creased with hasty
packing; she turned often to Pamela, drawing her into the
conversation; Pamela thawed a little, expanded about
rations, clothes coupons, petrol, David, and Arshaig, then
politely sulked again. On her clear brown cheek a flush
of resentment burned; behind her watchful eyes feelings
of hostility moved like sombre birds. This selfish, bad,
gambling woman could not seduce her for long.

Dinner was just over when Mrs. Cox came in.

"It's the young French boy, come to inquire about
Miss Barbary."

Pamela lifted her brows. "I thought the police had got him."

"His uncle bailed him out," said Sir Gulliver. "I imagine he will only be cautioned, as it's a first offence."

"A first offence in London, possibly," Helen murmured. "I'll go to him."

Raoul waited in the hall, nervous, small and unhappy. Seeing Helen, so little expected, he took a startled step back; she put out her hands to him; he came to her in sudden tears.

"Maman, maman . . ."

She held him to her. "Raoul, *mon petit*." After a moment she told him about Barbary. "She is very ill, and still unconscious. The doctor can't tell yet; but I think she will recover. Come to-morrow; come every day, if you like. Later we will talk; I want you to tell me about Barby—here they know nothing. You must see Roly too; I have brought him with me. Now you must go. Good night, my little son. I say it again, I think she will get well."

She returned to the dining-room.

"My stepson. I told him to come back whenever he wants to. He is, of course, very anxious and troubled."

Pamela hit out.

"Do we want him coming about the house? He's a thief, after all."

"So he is. So is Barbary. Unfortunately they must both be, for a time, about the house."

She left the room; they heard her going heavily upstairs.

Gulliver, without looking at his wife, said, in cold, level tones, "While Barbary is still in danger of death, perhaps

221

you would avoid speaking of her in a way meant to give pain to her mother and to me."

Pain ricochetted back, hitting Pamela straight on the heart like a physical blow; it was as if the child within her had been struck.

" Gully ! I never mentioned Barbary—what can you mean ? I was speaking about that boy. . . ."

" I know what you were speaking about, and so did Helen. I only ask you, while she is so critically ill, to refrain."

Grief, anger, jealousy, surged up together in Pamela's throat, choking her; she did not speak, for she could not have spoken without tears. She rose and left the room.

I must keep quiet, she told herself, fighting down sobs as she went upstairs. I mustn't give way or get excited, it will be bad for baby. She went into David's room and sat by his cot, praying. Oh, God, I can't bear it. Make her go away. Don't let him take her part against me, please, God. Let him love me best, me and David and baby. Oh, God, take Barbary to a hospital—the Middlesex—no, King's College, miles away at Brixton, so that she'll have to stay near it. Let it be like it was before; before she came, and before Barbary came.

Downstairs Richie and his father played chess. Sir Gulliver had to give Richie knights and castles and things; he remembered that he and Helen had always played level, and that it had been a toss up which won. Pamela would have needed both knights, both castles, the queen, and about half the pawns, so they seldom played. Pamela's games were really tennis and golf, at which she excelled.

222

At half-past ten Helen came down.

" The night nurse will be more comfortable without me," she said. " It isn't fair to stay; they relax so much better alone. She'll call me if there's a change."

Sir Gulliver had just won the second game. Richie offered his mother whisky and cigarettes.

" You're much too good for me, papa. So is mamma. She always beats me. Which of you beats the other? "

" We used to play pretty level." Sir Gulliver was putting the pieces away. Helen sat down opposite him.

" Do you feel like another game? I could do with one. It would take my mind off."

" Don't you think you had better get some sleep? "

" I couldn't sleep yet. I might in an hour or so. Will you play? "

" Very well."

" Five shillings? "

" As you like."

They played. Richie looked on, to improve his chess. It must have been still poor, for, at the end of half an hour, when Helen acknowledged mate, he could not see why. This long view on the part of chess players always seemed to Richie enviably smart. So did the running back over the game to see where the loser had gone wrong, which his parents often practised. But not to-night. Probably it was obvious to them both.

" I don't think," said Sir Gulliver, putting the board away, " that you can expect to be at your best to-night."

" No. No, I can't, of course. I think I would rather talk, if you have a little time."

He looked at her, meeting her eyes for the first time. In his, narrow and green like Richie's, was the cold, outraged pain of years, fighting with his sense of justice. To talk about Barbary—well, she had a right to that.

" Yes," he said. " I have time."

Richie said, " Well, I shall go to bed. Not that I like this going to bed so early; I agree with Florimel, it makes one so weary before morning. But I am still rocking from that dreadful plane. Good night."

" You want to talk about Barbary," Sir Gulliver told her, laying down the bounds beyond which conversation between them might not stray. " And I must say at once that I am very much to blame. I should not have let all this happen. I ought to have found some way. I neglected her too much from the first. I was very busy; she was difficult to approach. But I ought, of course, to have made it my business to discover how she was passing her time. And, after that business at Arshaig, when she ran away after taking money for her journey from a writing-table drawer, I ought not to have left her here alone with Mrs. Cox. She didn't want to come back to Scotland—I suppose naturally. But I ought to have stayed with her, or insisted on taking her away with me somewhere. I never won her confidence. I probably didn't try hard enough; and there were, of course, obstacles. . . . I supposed her busy all day at the Slade, or at her painting, when much of the time she must, according to Mrs. Cox, have been wandering about London with undesirable people she picked up, and with that boy. I blame myself very much. She was my responsibility, and I failed her; and so it has come to this.

The World My Wilderness

You must forgive me if you can. You know how little
good I am in any personal relationship."

Helen, lightly and gently, touched his hand; he withdrew
it as if her touch burned.

"My dear, it wasn't you who were responsible for
Barbary's way of life. I had her with me for the last seven
years; it was I who let her run wild."

"Yes," he agreed. "But you sent her to me, and she
became my business. We both neglected her, and perhaps
we ought both to apologise for it."

"It is I," she told him, "who must apologise to you for
Barbary, now and always." She paused, looking at him
gravely, seeming to weigh her words. Then she went on.
"But don't let us apologise for her now. All I can feel
about her is hope that she will live, and fear that she may
die. For the moment, that seems to fill my thoughts of
her. . . . What I do want to apologise for, though—among
all my major sins against you that can't be apologised for
—is this invasion of your household. It is hard on you and
on Pamela. Of course you must both hate it; don't think
I don't realise that. But, because Barbary is all that matters
to me for the time, I don't suggest going away. If Pamela
will put up with it for a time, it will be good of her. I'm
afraid it vexes her my having brought Roly; unluckily he
and David had a free fight when they met. And she dislikes
Barbary."

He winced a little at the forthright word.

"Hardly dislikes . . . they're not very compatible,
naturally."

"My dear, don't be so moderate. Of course she dislikes

225

Barbary; how shouldn't she? A person being dangerously ill doesn't cure dislike. But never mind that; it doesn't matter. Nor does it matter her disliking me. As to that, I don't see how she could help it. I'll keep the peace as well as I can. When is your child coming? "

" In November, I believe."

" All this disturbance must be bad for her. Well, it can't be helped. You must both try and forgive me and Barbary. What a mess it all is. Now I shall go to bed. It's strange to be sleeping in this house again. Nothing seemed less likely. I would have laid long odds against it, wouldn't you? "

" Very long. Good night."

He opened the door for her; when she had gone, he returned to his chair and read. He did not want to go upstairs till Pamela should be asleep; like Tancred's reverend tutor, he had " the mind of one unused to those passionate developments which are commonly called scenes."

* *31* *

DARKNESS and sickness engulfed Barbary; when not
darkness it was sickness, then it was darkness again.
Always, except when most deeply drowned in darkness, she
felt the pain in her wrenched back, not knowing what it
was. Faces and voices she did not know at all. She ran
down rocky corridors, leapt chasms, climbed steep stairs
up high towers, from which she sprang into space, her
hunters at her heels, squirmed into dark caves, to find the
Gestapo waiting for her in their depths, lay face downward
among rocks and bramble, pushing herself, Indian fashion,
along, was seized, bound, beaten, her arms twisted back,
matches lit between her toes. Always there was fear and
blackness and red pain. Sometimes she would blow up
trains, sometimes entice the enemy into a trap, sometimes
try to warn him, running in vain with weighted limbs.
Bats, hanging in caves and from church roofs, would gibber
and squeak; rats ran over her bound form; she lay trapped
deep in ruins, fearing death, fearing hell, trying in agony to
repent and be saved. Since there was no time where she was,
she did not know how it passed; since there was no fixed
place, she scampered over her dream universe unanchored;
an age to her might be to those who watched her merely

227

the turning of her head on the pillow, the breathing of a moan.

Then one morning she half-opened her eyes, looking heavily beneath drooping lashes at the wall beyond the bed's foot. She was, she perceived, in her own bedroom. Swivelling her glance painfully round, she saw her mother sitting there; and that seemed natural too, in that room; she was not surprised.

" Mummy," she weakly croaked; and then felt too tired to go on.

" Yes, darling." Helen's hand lightly touched her forehead, putting back the hair that strayed limply over it. " I'm here. But you mustn't talk much."

" Am I ill? " The solution occurred to her. She was ill, and her mother was looking after her. If she had been in the hands of the Gestapo, she was safe now. She sighed, and drifted drowsily into sleep.

The doctor, coming later, said it was now only a question of time; she would recover. Helen did not trust doctors; she knew that they lied. Her sister had died of cancer; the doctor had told them that it was not cancer, and that she would get better; she had died, and he had refused to show them the death certificate which would convict him of ignorance or deception. They had not said good-bye to her, or any last words; her death had taken them by surprise. If doctors could lie about such a thing, was any truth in them? Barbary might, for all she knew, be going to die to-night. She sat up with her all night, watching; heard the breath grow steadily more even, lighter, saw the restless movements quieten. By the morning, she had hope, and went to sleep, happy for the first time since the telegram had, like a bullet, shot into her heart. Barbary would recover.

Every afternoon Raoul called to ask after her, and sometimes to take Roly out into the embankment gardens to play. He introduced his half-brother to his uncle and aunt one day; they took a fancy to their little nephew in sin; he was just like Maurice, they said. Raoul was like his mother, and they had never been able to feel really warmly towards that quiet pale girl, so lacking in spirit and vivacity. But to see Roland's round, roguish face and smiling eyes looking up at them was to welcome their jolly brother once more into the family circle which he had always enlivened.

Presently both Roland and Raoul were allowed in Barbary's room for brief visits. By that time Barbary remembered, though fitfully, what had happened to her. She knew she had stolen from shops, been chased by police, seen Raoul caught, and had herself fallen from a wall.

Her mother told her Raoul had been released.

" Shall I be taken to prison ? " she asked.

Helen said no, they would certainly let her off as a first offender. " You see," she added dryly, " they fortunately don't know anything about your past."

Barbary agreed that this was fortunate. Had the Gestapo known all about her maquis activities, she would undoubtedly have been flung into gaol.

" All the same," said Helen, " you really mustn't go about stealing. It's most disreputable, and vexes your father very much. It disgraces him, you see. You shouldn't have taken

229

that money from Arshaig. That isn't the right way to behave in England; nor in Scotland either."

" No," Barbary admitted, her fingers playing with her mother's rings. She felt at peace, happy, restored to affection. Things were almost as they had been before. Yet not wholly, for a formidable question, never asked and never answered, loomed between them still.

" So," said Helen, " since you obviously don't know how to behave in Great Britain, I shall take you back to France directly you are well enough to travel."

Barbary's eyes opened wide.

" *Oh, mummy. Oh, yes.* Then I needn't ever come back here again, need I? "

" No, I don't see that you need, unless you want to. You can go on learning to paint in Paris. I shall probably live there part of the year, and go to the Fraises for the summer. Or I may let the Fraises and go somewhere else."

Barbary lay still and happy.

" Raoul? " she presently asked.

" Raoul is going to stay with his uncle in London. I'm sorry you two will be separated. But you'll make friends in Paris. And perhaps Raoul can come and stay with us sometimes."

Barbary, still holding her mother's hand, turned her face away, staring at the wall. All was still not right, with Maurice so grimly between them.

" Mummy," she said, speaking low and quickly, " we weren't there when Papa Maurice was drowned. Raoul and I weren't there."

Helen's hand had stiffened suddenly, lying rigid on the bed with Barbary's clasped round it.

"No? . . ." Question or acceptance, it fell oddly into the pause, empty of inflection.

"No," Barbary repeated, and her voice died faintly away. "Mummy, we weren't."

After a moment Helen said, drawing her hand gently from Barbary's: "I'm not asking you about it, Barbary. I know that your friends drowned Maurice; I've always known it. And that you and Raoul knew something about it. I don't want to know exactly how much you knew, or whether you could have stopped it, or saved him by warning him. I know you didn't want to give your friends away. But perhaps you hoped to save him somehow, and failed. Perhaps you left it till too late—I don't know what happened. I never told the police what I suspected, because I didn't want you dragged in. Nothing could bring him back. So I left it alone. I shall still leave it alone. I would rather not know more. It mattered between us once; but I don't mean it to matter any more. I don't think you or Raoul deliberately let Maurice be murdered; you were both fond of him and fond of me. I expect you lost your heads, wanted to save him, and didn't know how. Anyhow, now it's in the past, over and done, and it's no use brooding over it. . . . You and your friends thought Maurice was a *collaborateur*, didn't you. What a stupid word that is. He never betrayed anyone; all he did was to make the best of things and live in the world as it was, on terms with everyone round him, German and French. You all felt this was betrayal; perhaps it was; and God knows what else you thought he had done. So Maurice died. Poor Maurice, who was so kind and would never hurt anyone. . . . Well, that's over now. Except that I shall always miss him, and that Roly will grow up without a father. But life goes on, and you are as important to me as Roly is, and I'm not going to let you grow up without a mother. And now we won't ever talk of it again. We'll talk about Maurice, but not about his death. Stop crying, Barby. Think about going back to France with Roly and me, and painting in Paris, and the sea in summer. I hope Richie will often come out to us, too. And there's Maurice's cousin, Lucien Michel; he stays with me a great deal; you'll like him, I hope. So we shall all be happy, and there's nothing to cry about, and you know I never did let you, I would never have it. Where's your handkerchief, little nuisance? There, then."

"Oh, mummy, I do so love you."

"So do I you, as you know quite well. But we mustn't get soppy about it. Now I must go. By the way, you're hurting Coxy's feelings; she says you'll hardly speak to her when she comes to see you."

"No. . . . She's an informer. She set the police on us."

"Poor Coxy. She likes a little excitement."

"Well, she kept telling me not to trust people, and all the time it was *her* not to trust."

"Her and others. Of course. She was illustrating her own maxim. So I hope you *won't* go about trusting people. You can like them just as much without that. I trust no one myself. I'll tell Coxy she can bring you your tea."

32

Pamela had achieved a poise ; she went about with a mask of chilly politeness, off-hand, unsmiling, rather bored. She talked at meals, so far as she could, about things and people known to Gulliver and herself but not to Helen. But, what with Helen's conversational gifts and what with Richie's, it always turned out that Helen knew quite enough about them to keep up her end. The so-and-so's—were they still like that? Helen remembered the time when they had done this, said that; charmingly she endorsed and added to what Pamela said of them. Or Pamela would talk of food, clothes, shopping, the difficulties of housekeeping, and Helen contributed anecdotes from France. She could not be excluded; it was useless to try. She could make Gulliver smile, from out of his cold, deep resentment; she could induce in him his dry, sharp wit, so that the dinner table became, at times, an entertainment; a company dinner, Pamela called it in her mind and in her schoolgirl phrasing. It wasn't fair, it wasn't decent. Certain things had happened, and couldn't be passed over as if they hadn't. Helen had behaved like a bitch; now she was pretending to be an ordinary friend staying in the house and paying for her board and lodging by her entertainment value. Pamela

233

from time to time saw Gulliver's cold, shrewd eyes resting
on his divorced wife; she could not read their meaning,
she had little skill at that. That rich maturity of beauty, lost
to him for seven years—how did it affect him now? Did
it stab and stir his senses, did he desire her still, the intruder,
the revenante, returned to trouble him? In the house, he
avoided occasions of being alone with her; but did they
meet elsewhere? Helen, Pamela believed, had no scruples;
she would follow her desires into any forbidden territory,
and she might well desire Gulliver again, if only to pass
the time and prove her power. And he, an upright man,
was yet a man. Pamela tormented herself with suspicion,
fear and jealousy that worked themselves into hate. She
was proud, possessive, and deeply in love; even more than
she had known before this menace threatened. Jealousy of
the past years gnawed at her; those eighteen years of
Gulliver and Helen, together in this house, in these rooms,
in the life they had shared. By the side of that life, which
appeared so rich, so mellow, so full, so gay, so mature, the
life that he and she led now looked brittle and thin, her
own contribution to it adolescent. How could he, who had
loved and lived with an intellectual courtesan, be content
with a young woman so crude and uninformed as she? So
dull . . . the cruel word whispered itself like the cut of a
whip on her heart. If he had only married her because
Helen had left him, because he had to stanch his wound
and his hurt pride, because he needed a mistress in his house
and a hostess at his table, because she was young and nice
looking and adored him, and because he had the appetites
of a man. . . . And now here was the courtesan once more

come up out of the south like a ship in full sail, singing
her siren song, that was bitter as olives in the wife's ears,
but to the husband, what?

A wall as of glass rose between them; on her side of it,
Pamela felt helplessly alone. She had not even David, for
she had sent him to his grandparents to escape the menace
of Roland. Gulliver was courteous, absent, as if his mind
strayed somewhere beyond her reach.

With the lessening of anxiety Helen had bloomed into
gaiety. Her beauty shone richly magnificent, golden as a
September noon: it burnt into Pamela's nerves and senses,
a flame that seared.

Helen saw a few old friends; she went for a week with
Richie to Ireland, to stay with her father, a dispossessed peer
in Galway, who lived in the lodge of his burnt-out house
and kept racehorses; over seventy, he had lately married a
pretty young woman and had a baby, who was Richie's
step-aunt. Helen got on well with her gambling and racing
parent, who had been sorry, but by no means surprised,
when she had left that stiff fellow Deniston.

"Poor little Barbary," he said. "You must bring her
here when she's better, my dear. I could give her a nice
mount, and she could do just as she pleased. London's no
place for a growing girl."

"Thank you, Father, she'd love to come sometime.
But I shall take her back to France when she's well
enough."

"How's Gulliver?" He looked at her with curiosity,
the position being so odd. "And how do you get on with
his young woman?"

" As well as can be expected, I suppose. It's awkward for her, having me. And, of course, for Gully too. I must leave as soon as I can."

" You oughtn't to be there at all. It's outrageous."

" I suppose so. But Gully's used to that. Everything I've done to him has been outrageous."

She sighed. The past swept back at her, a ruthless, thriftless, smiling ghost.

" Well," said Lord Donwell, " it would be a pity to brood. No good ever came of that."

On this they were agreed; in point of fact, neither of them had ever tried it.

Helen returned to London to find Barbary sitting up and receiving visitors. Raoul came daily; he had no news of Horace, Jock or Mavis, who had deserted the ruins with the total flitting of startled animals.

" One does not imagine," said Raoul, in his innocent, experienced, cynical voice, " that one will see them again. They will, without doubt, in future carry on the underground movement elsewhere. As for me, I shall not return there either. It would not be amusing alone, and the police will be watching Somerset Chambers and the other residences we used. Besides, I have promised my uncle. For me the underground is finished. One cannot carry it on by oneself, and, anyhow, I shall for a time be under police vigilance."

" What shall you do, then ? "

" I shall collaborate. That is to say, I shall observe the laws, go daily to school, obey my uncle and aunt, attend mass on Sundays, keep out of the way of the police. Then they will perhaps let me visit you in France next year, as my stepmother has invited me."

" Yes, you must come. We shall be in Paris a good deal, maman says, as she wants me to go on with painting. She now has Lucien Michel a great deal with her, it seems. I don't care, so long as she lets me be with her too. Maman must have always a man. She has forgiven us for not saving papa Maurice, and one must accept this Lucien, who will make her happy, and who will not be always there, for he has not renounced his wife. So one will not fight against Lucien. But Raoul, one must not cry."

His hands were pressed to his eyes; tears shook him, for his jolly papa, whom they had not saved. Could they have saved him? Had he loved Raoul more, had Barbary felt no jealous resentment, Raoul no bitterness, would they have made the last desperate effort, have broken with their Resistance friends, if necessary betrayed them, and saved the collaborator?

" If one had been able to save him then," said Barbary, " he might still have been assassinated later, one must remember. Poor papa Maurice. I have cried too for him, and for maman; but now it is over and forgiven, and one must not cry any more. Maman says that. She has forgiven us both. If papa Maurice were here, he would forgive us too. He liked us to be happy and gay. And one supposes that he would like his cousin Lucien to console maman. So perhaps it has not ended so badly after all. Except for you, poor Raoul, who must stay in this dreadful London and go to school."

" Yes," he agreed. " London is dreadful."

They sat in silence, brooding over the dreadfulness of London and of life, which were, nevertheless, no worse than anyone who knew the world might rationally expect. Finding their way, with the instinct of jungle animals, to the waste places, the ruined holes, the rat alleys, the barbaric wrecked hinterland, which were what they recognised as home, they had found sustenance for their unhoping spirits there; exiled from this maquis, they breathed thinly the chilling air of life, that held, surely, nothing that concerned them.

"But, maman," said Barbary, and her face flickered as if a lamp were lit behind it, "will be home to-night."

* 33 *

A WEEK later Helen spoke to Gulliver for the first time about the future.

"The doctor thinks Barbary is well enough to travel now, Gully."

"Travel? Where to?"

They were sitting in his study; she had gone in to him at eleven o'clock, after Pamela had gone up to her room. Helen sat in a deep chair, just beyond the soft golden circle of the reading-lamp on the desk. Her firm white chin rested on one closed hand; her chestnut eyes looked deep and black beneath the broad pale brow. His heart turned over as he looked at her; his unslain passion surged in him like a great wave. He scarcely heard her words, only the rich deep voice like a cello, saying, "travel." Was she, then, to go from him again? Had that moment come? His eyes could not leave her face, her body, the curve of the hand that rested on her knee.

> But heart, there is no comfort, not a grain;
> Time can but make her beauty over again.
> Because of that great nobleness of hers
> The fire that stirs about her when she stirs

239

Burns but more clearly. O she had not these ways
When all the wild summer was in her gaze.
O heart! O heart, if she'd but turn her head
You'd know the folly of being comforted.

" To France. I had better take her back this week, I think."

At that he pushed his chair sharply back.

" Barbary is not going back with you to France. You know that. We must decide what to do with her; but if she is to grow into a decent, civilised young woman and member of society, she can't live in France. Not," he added, bitterly, " in *your* France."

" My France . . ." She echoed the words, as if she were speculating on the nature, the quality, of her France.

He informed her of them.

" Your France. The France of the comfortable collaborators and the disreputable maquis. The France of the rich opportunists and of the lawless criminals with which you let our daughter mix. . . . When you stayed on in France with Michel, it wasn't only me and Richie you were deserting, but the decency and integrity of the ordinary person. He was a collaborationist with the enemy occupying his country, with those disgusting barbarians who tortured and massacred and enslaved and abolished freedom and the rule of law. You lived with him, and tolerated the barbarians too. That shocked me more profoundly than your desertion."

" I see. But, you know, Maurice never collaborated, in the sense you mean. He never betrayed anyone to the

Germans or the Vichy police. He even sheltered escaped allied prisoners. All he did was to live in an occupied country and keep on amicable terms with its occupiers. Was there much harm in that ? "

He leant back, with a despairing gesture of the hand.

" The very fact that you can ask the question shows the gulf that there is between your attitude and the ordinary decent man's and woman's. The men Michel—and I presume you—were ' on amicable terms ' with were the brutal dregs of a community which had chosen the road to barbarism. If you *had* to stay in France, you should have refused to have even the slightest unofficial dealings with them. I gather that instead you and M. Michel used to exchange courtesies with them, and get, in return, some privileges."

" You are horribly well informed, Gully, as usual." She sighed; in her speculative look on him was ironic acceptance of the past and of his view of it.

" Of course," she said then, " you're less than just to Maurice, but how could you not be, in the circumstances ? And it is quite true that a nobler, more high-minded woman than I would have behaved differently. But you know of old that I was never noble or high-minded. Always selfish and self-indulgent, I'm afraid. So I took the easy road.

> It's human nature. Why, if so,
> Isn't human nature low !

Shall I tell you a thing that perhaps you *don't* know ? My poor, kind, easy Maurice, who never hurt anyone, whose only fault was amiability and acceptance of the arrangement his country had made with the enemy, acceptance, that is, of things as they were, was murdered by the maquis—drowned. So, you see, your principles were avenged, if that's any consolation to you."

"It is not. One crime avenged by another. As you should know, I am against crime. And it was with that very kind of criminal that you let our child run wild, till she became a natural outlaw and criminal herself. I have made up my mind to arrest that development, and you must let me do it in my own way."

"You've made up your mind. I see. Are neither I nor she to have any say in it?"

"You and I, I hope, will consult together about her education and future. She can state her wishes, so long as they don't include going back to you in France."

"As you know, they do."

"I do know it, too well. The child's whole heart is fixed on you, as it always has been. That is what makes your influence over her so dangerous."

"You fear she will grow up like me—lawless, self-indulgent, dishonourable."

"Not like you, poor child. She won't have your beauty, or the power to dominate people by her presence. She won't, heaven help us all, have that. It's just as well. I don't want another woman in my household going about with that outrageous power of inflaming. One is too many. One is more than I am able easily to cope with."

His voice had dropped; he leaned his forehead on his hand, not looking at her.

"I am very much in love with you, Helen. You are

quite aware of that. I ask myself if my decision to keep
Barbary has anything to do with wishing to keep a link
between us, to draw you back sometimes, so that I can see
and hear you occasionally. I know that if you take her
we perhaps may not meet again, anyhow for a long time.
But I don't honestly believe that my decision has a great
deal to do with that. With one part of my mind, I know
it is better that we shouldn't meet. I owe loyalty elsewhere,
and don't intend to betray it. That must seem odd to you,
I suppose, even though you wouldn't let me, in this case,
betray it, since you don't happen to want me. But I do
want you, extremely; so extremely that I couldn't answer
for the consequences if I saw much more of you. You
must go away, but you must leave our child with me till
she has grown into a more responsible creature."

If he had now met her gaze, he would have seen that it
held, mainly, compassion.

"Can nothing I say change your mind, my dear? Yes,
I know you have the custody, the legal right. But you will
be breaking Barbary's heart and spirit if you keep her from
me. I promise you, if you will let me have her, to do my
best for her. She shall work at painting in Paris, and I will
look after her. It was partly, you know, her jealousy of
Maurice that drove her to the maquis, poor child. I was
negligent, I admit it, and I'm sorry. Later, things came
between us . . . but never mind that now, it's over. I shall
look after her in future, and she will be happy. Here in
England, away from me, she will be unhappy."

"She will get over it. She will *have* to get over it, as I

243

shall. Perhaps we can help one another. No; I have made up my mind, and nothing you say will change it."

"*Nothing* I say?" She seemed about to speak; broke off, fell silent, sat still, as if she mused, her chin resting on one strong hand, her eyes speculatively on his bent head.

"In that case, my dear," she said presently—and her voice had dropped to a low, rich murmur, a tone that twisted his heart like a remembered tune—"in that case, we needn't speak of it any more. Argument between you and me—it never achieved much. There could be other things between us, Gully—I think there still are. Oh, my dear, can you forgive me, even a little?"

Leaning forward, she took his hand, drew it down from his face, made him meet her lustrous gaze. The waves rose, storming over him, sweeping away the brittle barriers, engulfing him.

"Forgive. . . . Oh Helen, Helen. . . ."

The years stood back : for how long, neither knew.

Presently Helen said : "Gully, we still care for each other. Must we go pretending we don't? Isn't that rather stupidly wasteful? Couldn't we be together sometimes for a little . . . perhaps in France? Would you care for it, my dear? Or would it be too . . . too ignoble for you to contemplate?"

Ignoble. The word sounded faintly through the engulfing seas that drowned his senses and heart.

"*Care for it* . . . my God, Helen, I care for nothing else : I've wanted nothing else since I saw you again. It's a madness that has captured about all of me. But we can't do it ; you know we can't, and we both know why.

Forgive me for forgetting it just now. I shouldn't have done it. I never meant to : it was unfair to both of us, and to Pamela. It's obvious that I can't trust myself to go on seeing you, and I mustn't."

" No ? " She saw the barriers being replaced again, the wall built up against the storming sea. This was more than the after-passion ebb that she knew of old : it was the resolution of his considered will, and would not break again. She would never win him, or win her child from him, that way.

" Loyalty," she diagnosed, sympathetically fingering qualities she knew to be his. " Loyalty and integrity." She sighed a little. " You are a very upright K.C., Gully. And, I'm afraid, incorruptible. Well, so that is that. . . . To return to Barbary—I still can't persuade you to give her to me, I suppose ? "

" No. You mustn't go on asking me, Helen. I can't do it, and don't intend to."

She knew that finality, knew that she had failed. Once more she sighed, not in renunciation, but in pity.

" I'm sorry . . . because you force me to play my last card, and to tell you something that I had hoped you would never need to know. You have several times spoken of ' our child.' But Barbary is not your child."

His face sharpened and whitened, like that of a man near death; he looked rigidly in front of him.

" So," he said coldly, " even then . . . Would it be in order to ask whose child she is ? I presume you are telling me the truth ? "

" Yes, I am telling you the truth. I'm sorry for making this Strindberg situation. As I said, I never meant you to know. But I can't lose Barbary, and have her made unhappy. She is my child, and I am responsible for her. I've done enough harm to her already, heaven knows. No other unhappiness is going to come to her through my fault. When she nearly died, when I believed she would die, I knew that she mattered to me more than anything else, and that she was mine to look after; my own little girl, whatever she's done, and whatever I've done. So you see, dear Gully, I had to tell you. . . . Whose child she is, you ask. Do you remember the summer I went to Spain to paint? It was 1928. Well, I met a Spanish artist at Tossa; we made friends, and finally went south to Torremolinos together for a month. He was called Vicente Rodriguez. We parted, and we haven't met since. For a time he wrote; but I never answered, and never told him about Barbary. I don't know if I was in love with him, exactly; perhaps he only excited me, by his painting and his—his Spanishness. And I, no doubt, excited him. Anyhow, ' what men call gallantry and gods adultery is much more common when the climate's sultry.' So there it was, and I and you were landed with his child. She has his skin and eyes, you know. I sometimes used to wonder if you would notice how unlike she was to you or me or Richie, or any of our relations. But you seemed to take her for granted, and I let it go at that. Now, at last, I can apologise for foisting her on you."

" Apologise." He repeated the inept word. " What do I reply? Not at all? Pray don't mention it? Or what?

. . . And you tell me this now, to-night, only a few minutes after . . ." He broke off, facing the cruel enormity that had happened to him, for a moment unable to speak. " May I ask," he said, using a careful, brittle control, " if your peculiar affection for her has been because you loved her father so greatly ? "

" I've told you, Gully, I'm not sure whether I loved him at all. Certainly not as I used to love you in our early years, before I began annoying you so much. No, I loved Barbary for herself; from the first time she looked up at me with those queer, slaty eyes of hers and smiled at me. And partly, I suppose, because she was entirely mine and no one else's. I always felt I had to protect her against the world and spoil her while I could. Of course I didn't protect her, poor baby; I let her run wild and get into all kinds of trouble, because I was too lazy and selfish and contented to bother. . . . And then I threw her off, threw her on to you. . . . But now I shall take care of her. Whatever other relationships I may have, she will come first. Before my little Roly, even—because he's going to be able to look after himself much better—and before everyone. She'll be mine for always. So you see, don't you, that I must take her away with me. In fact, now that I've told you this, I don't imagine that you'll want her."

" You are quite right. What I thought were my responsibilities obviously lapse. I do *not* want her. I don't want ever to see her or hear of her again. By all means take your Spanish daughter with you, and do exactly as you like with her; it has nothing to do with me. Your Strindberg act has been, as you see, a complete success. . . .

247

And that, I think, finishes our business to-night. You will be leaving England quite soon, I take it."

He stood up, waiting for her to rise. She, who had so often in the past seen him in this cold, bitter pallor of anger, stood up too, and for a moment they faced each other, their eyes level.

" I'm sorry, my dear," she said. " It's no use asking you to forgive me, for of course you can't, and why should you ? But perhaps later on you may be glad that I told you. It has lifted a tiresome responsibility from you, and, I expect, killed a tiresome love."

If it was a question, he did not answer it. Instead, he flung back a question at her.

" I suppose I am right in assuming that this Señor Rodriguez was one of a series. I am probably fortunate in not having had to rear and support a large family of—of stepchildren. No, don't tell me; I had rather not hear. A purely rhetorical question."

" All the same, I'll answer it. I think, in view of everything, that you have a right to know. Vicente was my second lover. I won't tell you who the first was; it would be unfair to him. After Vicente, I had no lovers until I met Maurice."

" I am surprised at your moderation. . . . Well, suppose we bring this very odd conversation to an end. I'll say good-bye as well as good night, as I shall be going away to-morrow by an early train. I shan't return here until I hear you are gone. I assume that this arrangement will be more comfortable for both of us, since ordinary intercourse would be a little difficult after this. It only remains for me

to congratulate you on the masterly success of a prolonged
fraud. If you hadn't happened to want your child yourself,
I take it you would, without a scruple, have saddled me
with her for life."

"I don't know, Gully." She seemed to weigh the
question, with objective detachment. "It's difficult to be
sure what one would have done in other circumstances.
Anyhow, now you'll be rid of us both for good. Anything
we may want to say to each other in future can be said
through Richie; he will be coming to see me often, I
hope."

"Richie. Oh, yes. He is, I believe, my son. He is said
to look like me, at least. Do you intend to tell him what
you have been telling me to-night?"

"I hadn't meant to. I had rather not. You will do as
you please about it; tell him if you feel he should be told.
I, as you know, am no judge of correct conduct."

"*I* tell him? Why should I? And how could I? I
never tell anyone anything; least of all a boy a thing like
this about his mother."

"No; of course you couldn't. I am glad. I dote on
Richie, and like to have his affection. And he's easily hurt;
he's not tough. I should like Barbary to go on having him
for a brother, too; he's very good for her; so civilising.
It stays between me and you, then, Gully."

She held out her hand to him; not taking it, he stepped
back and opened the door for her.

She went upstairs with a sigh. My poor dear Gully (she
thought), why did you drive me to drop that bomb?
(Or is it a bombshell when dropped metaphorically, and

what is the difference?) It would have been so much
easier to persuade you in a gentler way, and we should
both have enjoyed it. We did enjoy it, to-night. We're
both attractive still. Instead I've had to hurt you, and you'll
never get over it, and you'll hate me worse than ever before.
Odd, how much I mind that. I should like to have parted
in love not hate; or anyhow, in friendship. And who
would have been hurt by it? Not Pamela. She would
never have known: not for certain, and I think she half-
suspects us as it is, so it would have made no difference
to her. Poor Pamela, I must convince her before I go that she
needn't be afraid. One can't leave her in the pain of doubt.
Who *would* have been hurt, then? Only my poor Gully
and his honour. If *that* cracked, he might break up altogether,
I suppose. For him it would be like the black market, or
cheating the customs, or lying in court. As Richie would
say, he's far past forty, and has honour. Honour: what a
spiky, uncomfortable thing it can be. I expect the young
are wise to be dropping it. The young? What about me,
and Lucien, and nearly everyone we know? We all seem
what the seventeenth and eighteenth century writers called
" frail " in our virtue. " As frail as female virtue:" though
surely male virtue has always been even frailer, on the
whole. Gully, *vir probe et fortis*, you stand nearly alone, my
dear. Or is it just my ignoble world to whom you are so
alien? Is there another nobler world, where people like
you are common? I suppose I couldn't breathe in it . . .
and certainly Barbary couldn't.

Worlds flickered before her, strange, fantastic, amusing,
intimidating, remote. I am taking my child away from the

higher to the lower, she thought. But what have I or Vicente passed down to her that should make her a fit inhabitant of that rarefied air that Gully breathes? She would freeze in it and wither up. She must have sunshine, geniality, laughter, love; and if she goes to the devil she shall at least go happily, my poor little savage. *Damnosa hereditas*, of course Gully is thinking. He will be thankful to see and hear no more of her. I must go and see if she is asleep.

She entered the room softly; in the faint light from the street lamps Barbary lay sleeping, an arm beneath her head. Helen lightly touched the rounded olive cheek; she moved and sighed, and seemed smiling, as if her dreams were good.

Helen supposed that neither of them would ever be in this room, this house, again.

* 34 *

RICHIE, on the last afternoon of his vacation, walked home from Moorgate station across the ruins. Pausing at the bastion of the Wall near St. Giles's, he looked across the horrid waste, for horrid he felt it to be; he hated mess and smashed things; the squalor of ruin sickened him; like Flaubert, he was aware of an irremediable barbarism coming up out of the earth, and of filth flung against the ivory tower. It was a symbol of loathsome things, war, destruction, savagery; an earnest, perhaps, of the universal doom that stalked, sombre and menacing, on its way.

Autumn now lay sodden, with its drifting mists and quiet sunshine, on the broken city, on the companies' halls, where michaelmas daisies, milky ways of tiny blue stars, crowded among the withered rose-bay, the damp brown bracken, the sprawling nightshade and the thistles. Excavators had begun their tentative work, uncovering foundations, seeking the Middle Ages, the Dark Ages, Londinium, Rome. The Wall was being examined, its great bastions identified and cleared, their tiles and brickwork dated. Roman and medieval pots and coins were gathered up and housed; civilised intelligence was at work among the ruins. Before long, cranes and derricks would make their appearance, sites would be cleared for rebuilding, tottering piles would be laid low, twisting flights of steps destroyed. One day the churches would be dealt with, taken down, or mended and built up. The fireweed, the pink rose-bay, that had seeded itself in the burnt soil and flowed and blossomed everywhere where bombs had been, would take flight at the building and drift back on the winds to the open country whence it came, together with the red campion, the yellow charlock, the bramble, the bindweed, the thorn-apple, the thistle and the vetch. The redstarts and the wheatears, the woodpeckers and the hooting owls, would desert this wilderness too, and take wing for woods and fields. In place of the fireweed, little garden plots would flourish, gay with vegetables and flowers; the fire brigade already had one, trim and neat, with trenches of scarlet tomatoes, outside the Wall, and close to the old Jews' burying ground, which fair gardens and houses had covered four centuries ago. Beside the tomato garden a bonfire of weeds burned; sticks crackled and blue smoke drifted, smelling of incense and autumn.

So men's will to recovery strove against the drifting wilderness to halt and tame it; but the wilderness might slip from their hands, from their spades and trowels and measuring rods, slip darkly away from them, seeking the primeval chaos and old night which had been before Londinium was, which would be when cities were ghosts haunting the ancestral dreams of memory.

"I think," Richie murmured, "we are in rats' alley, where the dead men lost their bones."

Shuddering a little, he took the track across the wilderness

253

towards St. Paul's. Behind him, the questionable chaos of broken courts and lanes lay sprawled under the October mist, and the shells of churches gaped like lost myths, and the jungle pressed in on them, seeking to cover them up.

THE END

VIRAGO MODERN CLASSICS
&
CLASSIC NON-FICTION

Some of the authors included in these two series –

Elizabeth von Arnim, Dorothy Baker, Pat Barker, Nina Bawden
Nicola Beauman, Sybille Bedford, Jane Bowles, Kay Boyle,
Vera Brittain, Leonora Carrington, Angela Carter, Willa Cather
Colette, Ivy Compton-Burnett, E.M. Delafield, Maureen Duffy
Elaine Dundy, Nell Dunn, Emily Eden, George Egerton,
George Eliot, Miles Franklin, Mrs Gaskell,
Charlotte Perkins Gilman, George Gissing,
Victoria Glendinning, Radclyffe Hall, Shirley Hazzard,
Dorothy Hewett, Mary Hocking, Alice Hoffman,
Winifred Holtby, Janette Turner Hospital, Zora Neale Hurston
Elizabeth Jenkins, F. Tennyson Jesse, Molly Keane,
Margaret Laurence, Maura Laverty, Rosamond Lehmann,
Rose Macaulay, Shena Mackay, Olivia Manning, Paule Marshal
F.M. Mayor, Anaïs Nin, Kate O'Brien, Olivia, Grace Paley,
Mollie Panter-Downes, Dawn Powell, Dorothy Richardson,
E. Arnot Robertson, Jacqueline Rose, Vita Sackville-West,
Elaine Showalter, May Sinclair, Agnes Smedley, Dodie Smith,
Stevie Smith, Nancy Spain, Christina Stead, Carolyn Steedman
Gertrude Stein, Jan Struther, Han Suyin, Elizabeth Taylor,
Sylvia Townsend Warner, Mary Webb, Eudora Welty,
Mae West, Rebecca West, Edith Wharton, Antonia White,
Christa Wolf, Virginia Woolf, E.H. Young

JOANNA

Lisa St Aubin de Terán

*Not all mothers love their children, but few feel quite as negatively
about their offspring as Kitty does about Joanna. From the day the
big-boned, red-haired Joanna came into the world she has literally
had to fight for her life.*

So begins this powerful and haunting novel about three
generations of women living out an uneasy co-existence in the
wrong part of London. United by their desire to be somewhere
else, with other people, this is an extraordinary testament to
the blood-lines which tie family members to each other and
simultaneously wrench them apart.

THE GHOST STORIES

Edith Wharton

In these powerful and elegant tales, Edith Wharton evokes moods of disquiet and darkness within her own era. In icy new England a fearsome double foreshadows the fate of a rich young man; a married farmer is bewitched by a dead girl; a ghostly bell saves a woman's reputation. Brittany conjures ancient cruelties, Dorset witnesses a retrospective haunting and a New York club cushions an elderly aesthete as he tells of the ghastly eyes haunting his nights. Rich and strange, these stories reveal a seductive and little known aspect of this superb writer.

PLAYING THE HARLOT

Patricia Avis

Introduced by George H. Gilpin and Hermione de Almeida

'The thought of your great work makes me shudder' – *Philip Larkin to Patricia Avis*

Never before published, this dazzling *roman à clef* – by an angry young woman who knew most of the Angry Young Men of the 1950s – was rejected in 1963 by a distinguished publisher, partly 'because it slandered his friends', including Philip Larkin, with whom Patricia Avis had an affair. Here Mary Gallen, a gifted woman, but a drifting soul amongst the fifties generation of raffish male literary intellectuals, plays the harlot and measures her life in dry, unsparing wit; its poignancy foreshadowing the untimely death of the author.

MY ÁNTONIA

Willa Cather

Prefaced by A. S. Byatt

'The most sensuous of writers, Willa Cather builds her imagined world almost as solidly as our five senses build the universe around us . . . great is her accomplishment' – *Rebecca West*

Jim Burden tells the story of his beloved childhood friend Ántonia, the immigrant girl and woman whose struggle and splendour represent the source of life itself. Willa Cather sought to recapture the superb vitality of frontier America, nowhere more so than in this magnificent portrait of the pioneer woman, seen through the eyes of the man for whom she can only be a memory, never a possession.

LOVING WITHOUT TEARS

Molly Keane

With an introduction by Russell Harty

'Take any book by Molly Keane and I guarantee you will be delighted, warmed and sustained with pleasure . . . she is a born writer' – *Dirk Bogarde*

Angel, formidable hostess, social charmer and mother *par excellence*, confidently awaits the return of her little boy from the trials of war. Tightening the apron strings as she does so, she could not anticipate that the teenager who went away will return a grown man – bronzed and world-weary – sophisticated American widow on his arm. Nor could she anticipate that her irrepressible daughter Slaney will similarly throw herself into romance (without asking her advice) and even her niece Tiddley will show an unexpected determination in getting on with her life. Faced with domestic insurrection on a grand scale, Angel will have to sharpen her wits to maintain her tyranny. And sharpen them she will . . .

FULL HOUSE

Molly Keane

With an afterword by Caroline Blackwood

'Her books are witty, sardonic, human comedies, edged by black humour, and, like all good comedies, sadness and pathos lie close to the glittering surface' – *Polly Devlin*

Silverue – an enchanting Irish mansion – is owned by one of the most frightening mothers in fiction – the indomitable, oppressively girlish, Lady Bird. Blessed with wealth and beautiful children she has little to worry about except the passing of the years and the return of her son John's sanity. To help her through the potentially awkward occasion of John's return from the asylum she has enlisted the support and Eliza a woman she believes to be her confidante. But Eliza has her own secrets and John's homecoming will prove the catalyst for revelations which Lady Bird would much rather leave buried . . .

Virago now offers an exciting range of quality titles by both established and new authors. All of the books in this series are available from:

Little, Brown and Company (UK),
P.O. Box 11,
Falmouth,
Cornwall TR10 9EN.
Telephone No: 01326 317200
Fax No: 01326 317444
E-mail: books@barni.avel.co.uk

Payments can be made as follows: cheque, postal order (payable to Little, Brown and Company) or by credit cards, Visa/Access. Do not send cash or currency. UK customers and B.F.P.O. please allow £1.00 for postage and packing for the first book, plus 50p for the second book, plus 30p for each additional book up to a maximum charge of £3.00 (7 books plus).

Overseas customers including Ireland, please allow £2.00 for the first book plus £1.00 for the second book, plus 50p for each additional book.

NAME (Block Letters) ....

....

ADDRESS ....

....

....

☐ I enclose my remittance for ....

☐ I wish to pay by Access/Visa Card

Number ☐☐☐☐☐☐☐☐☐☐☐☐☐☐☐☐

Card Expiry Date ☐☐☐☐